# Unicorn Magic Discovering the Wonders of a Hidden World

Morgan B. Blake

Published by CopyPeople.com, 2024.

# Table of Contents

The Last Dreamer ..................................................................... 1
The Wishmaker's Secret ........................................................... 5
The Unicorn Who Couldn't Fly ............................................... 9
The Shifting Truth ................................................................... 13
The Last Horn .......................................................................... 17
The Midnight Pact ................................................................... 21
The Last Horn .......................................................................... 25
The Heart of the Hunt ............................................................. 29
The Midnight Circle ................................................................ 33
The Horn of Truth ................................................................... 37
The Last Gift ............................................................................. 41
Whispers of the Last Leaf ........................................................ 45
The Stolen Horn ....................................................................... 49
A Dream of Unicorns .............................................................. 53
The Tides of Fire and Light ..................................................... 57
Unicorn's Embrace ................................................................... 61
The Crystal Horn ..................................................................... 65
The Young Unicorn's Trial ...................................................... 69
Unicorn in the Snow ................................................................ 73
The Unicorn's Moonlight Ride ............................................... 77
The Unicorn's Last Dance ....................................................... 81
The Unicorn and the Lost Star ............................................... 85
The Forbidden Forest .............................................................. 89
Unicorn's Promise .................................................................... 93
The Unicorn and the Garden of Wishes ................................ 97
The Unicorn's Melody ............................................................. 101
The Dark Unicorn .................................................................... 105
The Unicorn's Island ................................................................ 109
The Unicorn's Eternal Love .................................................... 113
Unicorn's Shadow .................................................................... 117
The Moonlit Unicorn ............................................................... 121

The Thief and the Unicorn ................................................................ 125
The Silent Unicorn ............................................................................ 129
The Unicorn and the Enchanted Book ........................................ 133
Unicorn in the Wild ......................................................................... 136
The Golden Unicorn ........................................................................ 140
The Unicorn's Lullaby ..................................................................... 144
The Unicorn and the Magician ..................................................... 148
The Unicorn and the Butterfly ...................................................... 152
The Unicorn's Lost World .............................................................. 156
Unicorns of the Sea .......................................................................... 160
The Unicorn's Footprints ................................................................ 164
The Unicorn's Chosen One ............................................................ 168
The Unicorn's Cave .......................................................................... 172
Unicorn in the Mirror ..................................................................... 176
The Unicorn's Heart ........................................................................ 180
The Magical Unicorn Parade ......................................................... 184
The Dreamweaver and the Unicorn ............................................. 188
Unicorn in the Garden .................................................................... 192
The Return of the Unicorns ........................................................... 196
Get Another Book Free ................................................................... 200

Created by the CopyPeople.com[1]
All rights reserved.
Copyright © 2005 onwards .
By reading this book, you agree to the below Terms and Conditions.
CopyPeople.com[2] retains all rights to these products.

The characters, locations, and events depicted in this book are fictitious. Any resemblance to actual persons, living or dead, events, or locations is purely coincidental. This work is a product of the author's imagination and is intended solely for entertainment purposes.

All rights reserved. No part of this book may be reproduced, stored in a retrieval system, or transmitted in any form or by any means—electronic, mechanical, photocopying, recording, or otherwise—without the prior written permission of the publisher and the author, except in the case of brief quotations embodied in critical articles and reviews.

The views and opinions expressed in this book are those of the characters and do not necessarily reflect the official policy or position of the author, publisher, or any other entity. The author and publisher disclaim any liability for any physical, emotional, or psychological consequences that may result from reading this work.

By purchasing and reading this book, you acknowledge that you have read, understood, and agreed to this disclaimer.

- Thank you for your understanding and support.

**Get A Free Book At:** https://free.copypeople.com

---

1. https://copypeople.com/
2. https://copypeople.com/
3. https://free.copypeople.com

# The Last Dreamer

In a land untouched by time, where the sky shimmered with iridescent hues and the air was thick with magic, there lived a unicorn named Solara. Her coat sparkled with stardust, and her horn gleamed like the moon's first light. Yet, despite the beauty of her world, a sense of isolation gnawed at her. She had lived her entire life in the Emerald Glade, a lush valley hidden deep within the Silvermist Forest. The trees whispered secrets of the old magic, and the rivers sang songs of forgotten worlds. Solara had never known another of her kind.

One day, while wandering through the mist, she came across a gathering of the forest's creatures. A rabbit hopped nervously around the edges of the circle, while an owl perched atop a branch, silent and wise. But it was the fox, with its fur as red as the setting sun, who caught Solara's attention.

"You seek something, don't you?" the fox asked, its eyes gleaming with a knowing light.

Solara paused, taken aback. "What do you mean?"

"You've lived here all your life, alone. You've never seen another unicorn, and yet... you dream of it. You wish to find them, don't you?"

Solara's heart fluttered. She had longed to see another unicorn, to know that she wasn't the last of her kind. The idea of meeting someone who shared her story filled her with both hope and fear.

"I do," she admitted, her voice soft. "But... how can I find them? I don't even know where to begin."

The fox tilted its head, its fur shimmering like flames in the fading light. "You already know, Solara. The path is within you. You need only trust yourself."

With that, the fox vanished into the underbrush, leaving Solara to ponder its words. The next morning, she stood on the edge of the Glade, staring out at the vast expanse of the forest before her. The sun was just beginning to rise, casting a golden glow over the land, but it was the glint of something far in the distance that caught her eye. A faint, shimmering light—just like her own.

Her heart raced. Could it be? Could it be another unicorn?

Without hesitation, she set off toward the light, her hooves gliding effortlessly across the earth. As she journeyed, the landscape began to change. The trees grew taller, their branches twisting into intricate shapes that looked almost unnatural. The air thickened, charged with a palpable energy. Solara's senses tingled with anticipation.

After what seemed like an eternity, she reached the source of the light. A towering waterfall cascaded down a cliff, its waters glowing with an ethereal radiance. At the base of the falls stood a figure—a unicorn, just like her. The creature's coat shimmered in the mist, its horn radiating a soft, silver glow.

Solara's breath caught in her throat. For the first time in her life, she felt the presence of another unicorn. She stepped forward, her heart pounding in her chest.

"You've come," the unicorn said, its voice a soft melody that seemed to blend with the sound of the waterfall. "I've been waiting for you."

Solara blinked, astonished. "You were waiting for me? But how... how did you know I would come?"

The unicorn lowered its head, its eyes gleaming with an ancient wisdom. "I've always known. You see, Solara, you are not the last unicorn. You are the first."

The words struck her like a bolt of lightning. "The first?" Solara repeated, her mind reeling. "But... but I thought I was the last. The last of my kind."

The unicorn nodded, its silver mane flowing like a river of moonlight. "You were meant to be the first. Your existence, your presence, is the beginning of something much larger. The magic of the unicorns has been dormant for centuries, but it is time for it to awaken once more. You were born to carry that magic forward."

Solara took a step back, overwhelmed by the revelation. "But... I've never met another unicorn. I've lived my life in solitude. How can I be the first when I've never known anyone like me?"

The unicorn smiled gently. "Because the world was not ready for the magic of unicorns until now. You were meant to discover your own power, your own worth. Only when you believed in yourself, when you embraced your own uniqueness, would the magic return. Now, it is time for you to lead the way."

Solara's mind swirled with confusion and awe. She had spent her entire life searching for others, longing to find her place in the world, only to learn that her purpose was not to find others, but to be the spark that would ignite a new era for unicorns.

"But... I don't know how to lead," she whispered, doubt creeping into her voice.

The unicorn stepped closer, its presence calming and reassuring. "You've already led, Solara. By seeking, by yearning, you've already begun the journey. Now, you must share that journey with the world. The magic is inside you, just waiting to be unleashed."

For the first time in her life, Solara understood. She had been searching for something outside herself, when the true power had always been within. Her quest had not been about finding others; it had been about finding herself.

The unicorn gave her one final smile before turning and stepping into the glowing mist of the waterfall. As Solara watched it disappear, she realized that her journey had only just begun.

With newfound clarity, Solara returned to the Emerald Glade, not with the expectation of finding another unicorn, but with the knowledge that she was the beginning of something new. She was the keeper of a forgotten magic, and it was up to her to share it with the world. As the sun rose higher, casting its warm light over the land, Solara felt the stirrings of something deeper within her—a magic ready to be unleashed, a magic that would change everything.

And so, the last unicorn was no longer the last. She was the first of many to come.

# The Wishmaker's Secret

In the heart of a dense, untamed forest, there existed a place where the earth whispered secrets and the wind carried ancient tales. Few had ever ventured deep enough into its shadows to discover its hidden treasures, and fewer still returned to tell of what they had found. For a long time, it was believed that this forest was merely a figment of myth—an enchanted realm where only the bravest dared to tread. But for one curious child, the forest held a different kind of promise.

Kara was no ordinary child. From a young age, she had been fascinated by the stories her grandmother would tell her by the fire—tales of magic, of creatures from forgotten times, and of wishes that could be granted by those who truly believed. Kara, unlike most children her age, believed wholeheartedly in these stories. She spent countless days wandering the edges of the forest, hoping to catch a glimpse of one of the wonders her grandmother had described.

One bright spring afternoon, with the sun high in the sky and the air buzzing with the scent of pine and wildflowers, Kara wandered farther than she ever had before. The familiar path she had walked on countless occasions suddenly seemed to disappear beneath the thick underbrush. The trees were taller here, their twisted branches stretching out as if they were trying to hide the very sun itself. Yet, something tugged at her heart, a pull deeper than curiosity—a whisper calling her deeper into the forest.

As she ventured deeper, the forest seemed to shift around her, as if it were alive, watching her every move. Then, as if stepping into another world, Kara came upon a small clearing. The air here was thick with magic, and the center of the clearing was bathed in a soft, ethereal light. And there, standing in the middle of it all, was a unicorn.

The creature was unlike any she had ever seen, its coat gleaming like polished ivory, its mane flowing like liquid silver. Its eyes, deep and knowing, locked onto hers. Kara's heart skipped a beat as she stepped forward, unsure of what to do. The unicorn lowered its head, its horn catching the light in a way that made it sparkle like a thousand stars.

"You've come," the unicorn said, its voice musical and soft, yet carrying a weight of ancient wisdom. "I've been waiting for you."

Kara's mouth went dry. "W-waiting for me?"

"Yes," the unicorn replied, its gaze steady. "I am the last of my kind, and I have the power to grant one wish. But only to one who is truly deserving."

Kara felt a mixture of disbelief and excitement. She had heard of such creatures in her grandmother's stories, but she never imagined one would be real—let alone standing before her, offering to grant a wish. The possibilities were endless. Her mind raced with ideas: a wish for endless riches, or maybe the power to fly.

"What do you wish for, child?" the unicorn asked, its eyes searching Kara's face as though it could peer into her very soul.

Kara hesitated, caught between the endless possibilities and the sudden awareness that this was a moment that would define her life. She thought of her family, of the struggles they had faced, and of the world around her—so much hurt, so much yearning. She could wish for something for herself, but that didn't feel right.

"I wish for peace," she said quietly, her voice trembling. "For my family, for the world... for everyone."

The unicorn's eyes softened, and it stepped closer, its hoofprints leaving glowing trails on the earth. "A noble wish, indeed," it said, lowering its head once more. "But I must warn you, child, wishes come with consequences. You are not prepared for what you ask."

Kara felt a chill run down her spine. "What do you mean?" she asked, suddenly uncertain.

The unicorn did not answer immediately. Instead, it stared at her, and for a moment, the world seemed to stop. Then, in a voice barely above a whisper, the unicorn spoke.

"I have granted many wishes in my time, and all have come with a price. The wish for peace you ask for will not bring what you think. True peace, child, is not something that can be given—it must be earned. The very nature of your wish will change you, shape you into something you may not recognize. Once you make this choice, there is no turning back."

Kara stood still, her heart racing. "But... I want peace. For everyone."

The unicorn's eyes, ancient and wise, met hers. "Peace is an illusion, child. You may wish for it, but you cannot control how it will manifest. The world is a balance of light and shadow, and your wish will tip that balance in ways you cannot foresee. Are you sure this is the path you want to take?"

Kara swallowed hard, the weight of the unicorn's words sinking deep into her heart. She had come for a wish, for something that would make everything better, but now, she wasn't so sure. The unicorn was right—there was no easy path to peace. And what if her wish changed the world in ways she couldn't predict? Was she prepared to face those consequences?

"I..." Kara began, her voice faltering. "I don't know."

The unicorn stepped closer, its breath warm against her skin. "There is a reason why wishes are not granted lightly. They are powerful, yes—but they come with a burden that even the purest heart may not bear. You have the choice, child. You may wish for peace... or you may choose another path."

Kara closed her eyes, her mind swirling with thoughts and fears. After a long moment, she opened them again, her decision clear.

"I choose to walk my own path," she said, her voice steady. "I will work for peace, not wish for it."

The unicorn nodded slowly, its eyes filled with approval. "A wise choice. For peace cannot be granted—it must be built, day by day, with love, understanding, and sacrifice. You have learned a lesson, Kara, one that few ever understand. And that lesson is your true gift."

As Kara turned to leave the clearing, she felt a strange sense of peace wash over her—not the kind that came from a wish, but the kind that came from knowing that the journey was hers to shape. The unicorn's words echoed in her mind as she made her way back to the forest's edge, the world suddenly feeling more vast, yet more within her reach.

And as the sunlight bathed her face, she realized that sometimes, the hardest path was the one that led to self-awareness. The wish, in the end, wasn't about what could be granted—it was about what could be earned.

# The Unicorn Who Couldn't Fly

In the heart of the Glimmering Wood, where the trees shimmered with the light of magic, there was a young unicorn named Sylas. From the moment he was born, his coat gleamed with the purest white, and his horn spiraled like a silken thread of moonlight. Yet, there was something missing—something that all the other unicorns in the Glimmering Wood had. Sylas was born without wings.

The wings were a symbol of grace and power, a gift that every unicorn was given upon reaching maturity. It was said that only those truly destined for greatness could earn their wings. And yet, Sylas had grown into adulthood without ever sprouting even the faintest trace of feathers.

As the years passed, Sylas watched his fellow unicorns soar through the sky, their wings catching the breeze as they glided above the trees. He watched them dance on the clouds, their laughter echoing in the wind. Every unicorn was born with a spark of magic, but the wings—the wings were the ultimate sign of that magic. And Sylas felt that he lacked it.

He tried, of course. He had practiced for hours each day, running through the fields and stretching his legs in hopes that one day he might just lift off the ground. But no matter how hard he tried, his hooves never left the earth. His friends would cheer him on, but they all secretly knew that a unicorn without wings was incomplete.

Sylas couldn't help but wonder what it was that kept him grounded. Was he not special enough? Was his magic not as strong? As the days went by, he grew quieter and more withdrawn. He would wander the edges of the Glimmering Wood, staring up at the other unicorns, wishing he could join them.

One day, while sulking by the Moonlit Stream, Sylas encountered an old, grizzled unicorn named Vael. Vael was ancient, with a coat that had faded into a soft, silver-grey and eyes that sparkled with a deep wisdom. His wings were large and proud, a sight to behold. Yet, he did not fly. Instead, he stood still, watching the world from the earth with a peaceful contentment.

"You're troubled, young one," Vael said, his voice rough but kind.

Sylas hesitated. "I don't have wings," he admitted, looking down at his hooves. "I've tried everything, but no matter what, I can't fly. I'll never be like the others. I'm... incomplete."

Vael's gaze softened, and he slowly walked over to the stream, settling beside it. "Let me tell you a story," he began. "When I was young, I too longed for flight. I was born without wings, much like you. And I thought, just as you do, that without them, I would never truly be magical. But one day, I realized something: wings are not the only way to touch the sky."

Sylas tilted his head, confused. "What do you mean?"

Vael smiled, his eyes distant as if lost in a memory. "Magic is not defined by how high you can fly. It's not about what others see, but about what you feel inside. For years, I tried to fly, and each failure brought more frustration. But eventually, I stopped trying. I focused on my magic, not the wings, and I began to see the world differently. I realized that I could soar in ways that the others could not. I could see the beauty of the earth, the roots of the trees, the flow of the rivers. And that was enough."

Sylas listened intently, but the weight of his doubts lingered. "But I don't have wings. How can I be magical without them? How will others see me?"

Vael chuckled softly. "Your wings are not the measure of your worth, Sylas. It's your heart, your spirit. If you truly believe in your own magic, others will see it too. Perhaps your magic lies elsewhere."

Sylas sat in silence, pondering Vael's words. He had always believed that without wings, he was incomplete. But now, for the first time, he considered the possibility that there was another kind of magic he had overlooked—the magic of simply being himself.

Days passed, and Sylas continued to practice his magic in new ways. He spent time in the meadows, listening to the wind and learning the language of the birds. He spent hours by the Moonlit Stream, watching the reflections of the stars and learning to manipulate the water with his horn. It wasn't the magic of flight, but it was magic nonetheless.

Then one evening, as the sky painted itself in shades of orange and pink, Sylas stood at the edge of the Glimmering Wood, his eyes fixed on the horizon. The other unicorns were flying above him, their wings spread wide as they soared through the air. But Sylas did not feel envy. Instead, he felt a calm that he had never known before. His hooves were firmly planted on the ground, yet his heart felt light as a feather.

He closed his eyes and whispered a silent wish: "I don't need to fly. I just want to be me."

And in that moment, something extraordinary happened. Sylas felt a surge of energy rise from within, a magic so pure and powerful that it radiated through the very earth beneath his hooves. He felt connected to everything—the trees, the wind, the river, and the sky. He was a part of it all, just as much as the unicorns who flew above him. The world felt alive, and for the first time, Sylas realized that his magic had always been here, within him.

As he opened his eyes, he saw Vael standing nearby, watching him with a knowing smile. "You've found it, haven't you?" Vael asked.

Sylas nodded, his heart swelling with a newfound understanding. "Yes," he said softly. "I don't need wings to be magical. I am magical, just as I am."

Vael smiled, his eyes twinkling with pride. "Exactly, young one. You have discovered the greatest magic of all—the magic of self-acceptance."

And from that day forward, Sylas no longer wished for wings. He did not need them to be complete. He was magical in his own way, and that was more than enough. As the sun dipped below the horizon, casting its last golden rays across the land, Sylas stood tall, a unicorn who had learned that sometimes the greatest magic is simply being true to oneself.

# The Shifting Truth

In a secluded valley where the trees grew taller than any human imagination could fathom and the sky shimmered with a hue not seen anywhere else in the world, lived a unicorn named Aeris. He was not like the other unicorns of the valley—those who pranced about with gleaming horns, their manes flowing in the breeze, and their wings catching the sunlight like rays of starlight. Aeris possessed something unique—an extraordinary gift, or perhaps, curse: the ability to shapeshift.

At first, his transformations were subtle. A flick of his horn, a shimmering of his silver-white coat, and he could turn into a bird, a wolf, or even a cloud drifting across the sky. Aeris had always been fascinated by this power. The idea of being anything he wanted, of slipping into different skins, was thrilling. But as time passed, he began to feel something—something strange and unsettling. It wasn't the thrill of becoming another creature that began to weigh on him, but the realization that he could never quite feel at home in the forms he took.

When Aeris first shifted into the shape of a wolf, he thought it would be a magnificent experience. He imagined himself running alongside the other wolves, howling at the moon with the pack, feeling the pulse of the wild coursing through his new body. But when the transformation was complete, and he opened his eyes to the dark forest around him, he felt... disconnected. The wolves didn't see him as one of their own. They sniffed at him, unsure, before running off into the night.

The same thing happened when Aeris tried being a bird. The other birds fluttered around him, chirping their songs, but they never accepted him as one of them. He could mimic their songs perfectly, soar through the sky with ease, yet he felt like an outsider in their world. No matter what form he took, he was always just a visitor, a stranger passing through, never quite fitting in.

One day, as Aeris wandered the valley, lost in thought, he came across a gathering of forest creatures. They were all around a shimmering pond, laughing, talking, and playing. There were deer, foxes, rabbits, and even a few owls perched in the trees. Aeris watched them from the shadows, feeling an intense longing.

He had seen the other creatures live in harmony before, but never had he felt so desperately out of place. He wanted to join them, to be a part of their carefree world, but he knew that if he revealed himself, they would treat him like all the others—someone who didn't belong.

He could feel the stirrings of magic within him. With a quick thought, he shifted into the form of a deer, sleek and graceful. His hooves made no sound as he approached the group, blending seamlessly into their midst. The creatures glanced at him with mild curiosity but accepted him into their fold. They greeted him with warm nods and kind smiles. For a moment, Aeris thought he had finally found where he belonged.

But even as he walked with them, his heart heavy with this new form, something felt wrong. He was moving with their steps, grazing alongside them, and yet there was an empty space within him that nothing could fill. He wasn't truly a part of their world. He wasn't really a deer. He was simply pretending, slipping on the skin of another creature like a costume that didn't fit quite right.

Days passed, and Aeris grew tired of his shapeshifting ways. No matter how many times he shifted into different forms, he could never escape the loneliness that accompanied him. His transformations no longer brought the joy they once had. They only deepened his sense of displacement. He began to wonder if there was something wrong with him. Was he not meant to belong anywhere?

One evening, as he stood on the edge of the valley, looking out at the distant horizon, Aeris heard a voice—a voice as soft and gentle as a breeze, yet carrying the weight of centuries of wisdom.

"You've been searching for your place, Aeris," the voice said. "But you've been looking in the wrong way."

Aeris turned to find an old owl perched on a nearby tree. Its feathers were a mixture of gold and silver, and its eyes glowed with an ancient knowledge.

"I've tried to belong," Aeris said, his voice heavy with frustration. "I've taken so many forms, but I never feel at home. No matter what I become, I am always an outsider."

The owl tilted its head, considering Aeris's words. "You've been searching for something outside yourself. But your true place isn't defined by the shape you take or the form you wear. It's within you."

Aeris stared at the owl, confused. "What do you mean?"

The owl's voice softened. "The magic that flows through you, the ability to change into any form you wish—it is a gift, yes. But it's also a reflection of something deeper. You don't need to change to find your place, Aeris. Your true home is not in the form you wear, but in the truth you carry with you."

Aeris's heart thudded in his chest. "The truth I carry with me?"

The owl nodded. "You've been trying to fit into the world by changing yourself. But the world is not meant to be molded to your desires. It is meant to be embraced as it is. And you, too, must embrace yourself as you are. Not as a deer, or a bird, or any other creature—but as Aeris. You have been running from the truth of who you are, thinking you can change to fit in. But the only form that matters is the one you are born with. When you accept that, you will find your place."

Aeris stood there, speechless, as the owl's words echoed in his mind. For the first time in his life, he understood. He had spent so much time trying to change himself, to become someone he wasn't, that he had forgotten the power of being who he was. He wasn't a deer or a wolf. He was a unicorn, and that was enough.

The owl smiled, its eyes gleaming. "You'll find that when you stop changing, the world will change with you."

With that, the owl spread its wings and flew off into the night, leaving Aeris standing in the soft glow of the moon.

From that day forward, Aeris no longer felt the need to shapeshift. He accepted himself as he was—unique, magical, and whole. And in doing so, he found that his place in the world had always been there, waiting for him to step into it, just as he was. The creatures of the valley no longer saw him as an outsider. They saw him for who he truly was: Aeris, the unicorn who didn't need to change to belong.

# The Last Horn

The city was buzzing with the usual chaos of midday traffic. People darted through the streets, their eyes glued to their phones, hurrying from one place to the next. The hum of the modern world drowned out everything else—until it didn't. It started with the sound of hooves, sharp and rhythmic, echoing off the towering glass buildings. At first, it was so surreal that no one thought much of it, but then the air seemed to thicken. People stopped, their eyes lifted, and what they saw left them frozen in disbelief.

There, standing in the middle of Fifth Avenue, was a unicorn. Its coat shimmered like moonlight on water, and its long, spiraling horn gleamed with an almost otherworldly glow. The creature stood still for a moment, eyes wide and bright, scanning the busy city as if it had just stumbled out of a dream. For a brief instant, time itself seemed to halt.

And then, pandemonium erupted.

Screams filled the air as people whipped out their phones, snapping pictures, recording videos, some even yelling in excitement. The unicorn, caught in the frenzy, turned its head nervously. Its hooves clicked against the pavement, echoing in the unnatural silence. It was majestic and beautiful, but there was an edge of panic in the way it paced back and forth, as though it knew this was no place for something like it.

Miranda, a young woman in her twenties, was among those who stopped, her eyes wide with disbelief. She couldn't help herself. She moved closer, slowly, drawn to the creature. It was the kind of magic you read about in fairytales, yet here it was, standing in the middle of the modern world. But as she got closer, her excitement morphed into a sharp awareness. Something wasn't right. The unicorn didn't look like it belonged here—not just because of its horn or its glittering mane, but because of the nervous energy it exuded.

And then she saw them. A pair of dark-suited figures in the crowd, their eyes trained on the unicorn, moving with purpose. They weren't looking at the spectacle the way everyone else was—they were looking at it as if they were hunting it.

The unicorn bolted, its legs moving with a speed that was almost too fast for the human eye. It galloped down the street, its hooves striking the concrete, causing a wave of confusion in its wake. The suited figures began chasing it, and Miranda felt a wave of dread settle over her chest. She couldn't just watch this creature being chased through a concrete jungle—it wasn't right. It was magical, something sacred, and it belonged to the wild, not to be corralled into a cage or exploited for someone's gain.

Without thinking, she ran after it. She knew the city like the back of her hand, but she didn't know where the unicorn was headed. The suited men were gaining ground, and she could hear them shouting orders at one another as they pushed past pedestrians. Miranda couldn't let them catch it. She couldn't let anyone take away this piece of magic.

Through alleyways and across busy intersections, she ran, the unicorn's silhouette just ahead, the suited men still on its trail. It was as if the creature could sense the danger. Each time the men came closer, the unicorn seemed to leap higher, faster, more desperately. It was cornered, and so was she. They had reached the edge of the city, the towering buildings giving way to a large, fenced-off park, a dead end.

Miranda slowed, breathless, realizing she had nowhere else to go. She watched in horror as the suited men approached the unicorn, who was now backed up against the fence, its breathing heavy and frantic. The men raised their hands, calling for reinforcements, and Miranda knew it was over. But then, something strange happened. The unicorn stood still, its eyes meeting hers. It wasn't afraid anymore. Its horn began to glow, first faintly, then with growing intensity, until it seemed to hum with energy, sending ripples through the air.

The men faltered, as if caught in the creature's gaze. They tried to step forward, but they couldn't. There was a tension in the air, a force neither of them had anticipated. And then, in a sudden flash of light, the unicorn vanished.

Miranda stumbled, her heart pounding. One moment, the unicorn was there—majestic and alive—and the next, it was gone, as if it had never existed. The suited men stood frozen, their eyes scanning the empty space where the unicorn had stood moments before. They looked at each other, then at Miranda, before walking away, defeated.

As they disappeared into the city, Miranda stood alone, still processing what had just happened. She couldn't believe it. The unicorn hadn't just disappeared—it had done something. It had made them leave. And yet, she didn't understand how or why. It wasn't until she looked down at the pavement that she saw it—a small, golden feather resting by her feet.

Miranda bent down to pick it up, running her fingers over the smooth surface. She held it in her palm, feeling its warmth. It was no ordinary feather. It was magic—unmistakable and pure. She could feel its power thrumming through her veins.

As she stared at the feather, something shifted inside her. The world around her, the one so steeped in technology and modernity, felt less real somehow. In that brief moment of connection with the unicorn, she realized something—magic wasn't meant to be controlled, contained, or owned. It was meant to be free, to roam where it could, to elude those who would try to harness it for their own purposes. The unicorn had vanished, not because it was scared, but because it had made a choice to protect itself. The magic had always been more powerful than the cages that people tried to build around it.

Miranda tucked the feather into her pocket, her fingers trembling. As she walked back into the city, the streets no longer seemed as crowded or as loud. She knew something that no one else did—that magic was real, and that it had a purpose beyond human understanding. Maybe the unicorn wasn't meant to be captured. Maybe it wasn't even meant to be found. But for a brief moment, it had been part of the world—part of her world.

And just like that, the city felt a little smaller, a little less distant, as if, for the first time, it had allowed a piece of the impossible to slip through the cracks.

# The Midnight Pact

The Enchanted Forest had always been a place of harmony, where creatures of every shape and size coexisted beneath the canopy of ancient trees, their branches intertwined like old friends. Magic swirled in the air, so thick that it could be tasted on the tongue. The forest's heart beat with the rhythm of the earth itself, alive with the whispers of forgotten spells and the songs of unseen creatures. But recently, a shadow had begun to creep through the trees, a darkness that no one could explain but everyone could feel. The harmony was faltering.

In the deepest part of the forest, where the trees grew so tall they pierced the sky, a unicorn named Lira galloped through the mist. Her white coat glimmered with a soft, ethereal light, and her horn was a spiraled beacon of hope. She had long been the protector of the forest, guarding its magic from the forces that would seek to corrupt it. But today, something was different. The forest felt heavier, the air thick with an ominous tension. She could sense the disturbance—the darkness was growing stronger.

Lira stopped at the edge of a clearing, where a circle of ancient stones marked the meeting place of the forest's most powerful beings. The trees here were twisted, their bark scarred from some unseen force. At the center of the stones stood the Fairy Queen, Aradia, her wings shimmering with an otherworldly glow. Her emerald eyes locked onto Lira's with a mixture of urgency and sorrow.

"You've felt it too, haven't you?" Aradia's voice was like the wind through the leaves, gentle but laced with concern.

Lira nodded, her heart heavy. "The darkness is spreading. It's consuming the heart of the forest. I can feel it in every leaf, every root."

Aradia's wings fluttered, and she stepped closer to the unicorn. "I fear it may be too late. Something—someone—is drawing power from the deepest part of the forest. The ancient magic is being twisted, and if we do not stop it soon, it will destroy everything."

Lira's ears perked up. "Do you know who it is?"

Aradia hesitated, her gaze flickering with doubt. "It's an old enemy, one who has been hiding for centuries. A dark sorcerer, once banished from this land, has returned. His name is Malgor, and he has found a way to tap into the forest's magic. If we do not act quickly, he will consume it all."

Lira's heart pounded. Malgor was a name whispered in fear by the creatures of the forest. A sorcerer who had once tried to seize the magic of the land, he was banished after a great battle centuries ago. But now, he had returned, and the forest's very life was at stake.

"We can't fight him alone," Lira said, her voice firm. "But together, we might stand a chance."

Aradia nodded, her eyes glowing with determination. "We must combine our powers. I can call upon the magic of the forest's creatures, but I need you to lead them. Your strength and your heart are what will give us the edge. But there is one thing you must know—this will not be an easy battle. The darkness Malgor has unleashed feeds on fear, and it will seek to break us from within."

Lira's muscles tensed. The forest was full of light and life, but the shadows were spreading, and the fear they carried was insidious. She had always fought for what was right, but this... this felt different. The stakes had never been so high.

Together, the unicorn and the Fairy Queen ventured deeper into the forest, gathering the magical beings who called it home. From the talking animals to the ancient trees, all were drawn to the call of Aradia's wings. The forces of the forest assembled—together they would fight, but it would take more than just magic to overcome the threat of Malgor's darkness.

The final confrontation took place at the heart of the forest, where the ancient tree, the source of all magic, stood. The tree was dying. Its once vibrant leaves had turned to ash, and its branches hung limp. In the center of the clearing stood Malgor, his dark cloak flowing around him like smoke, his eyes gleaming with malice. His presence alone was enough to send chills down Lira's spine.

"I knew you would come," Malgor's voice was low, filled with cruel amusement. "But it's too late. The magic of this forest is mine now."

Aradia stepped forward, her wings aglow with the collective magic of the creatures who had gathered. "You will not destroy this land, Malgor. Its magic is not yours to take."

Malgor laughed, a cold, hollow sound. "You are weak, Fairy Queen. The magic you've gathered is nothing compared to what I have now. The forest is mine, and soon, all of it will bend to my will."

Lira stepped forward, her horn glowing brightly. "Not if I have anything to say about it."

The battle that ensued was fierce. Malgor's dark magic clashed against the combined forces of the forest. Aradia summoned the wind, the earth, and the creatures of the woods to fight back, but Malgor's power was overwhelming. Lira charged forward, her horn alight with energy, but the closer she got, the more she felt the fear creeping into her heart. The shadows whispered in her mind, doubt clouding her thoughts.

Just when it seemed like all hope was lost, something changed. The fear Malgor had planted in her heart began to fade. Lira realized that the true strength of the forest was not in its magic, but in its connection to those who cared for it. The unicorn closed her eyes, grounding herself in the earth beneath her hooves. The forest was not just a place of magic—it was a community, a living, breathing entity that thrived on love, respect, and unity. And that, Lira realized, was the key to stopping Malgor.

With a surge of strength, Lira's horn erupted with brilliant light. The magic of the forest, fueled by the love and loyalty of all its creatures, joined with her own power. Together, they created a shield of pure energy that repelled Malgor's darkness. He screamed in frustration as his power was stripped away, his form disintegrating into nothingness.

When the battle was over, the forest was silent. The ancient tree began to bloom once more, its leaves green and full of life. The magic of the land was restored, and the creatures gathered, their hearts full of gratitude and joy.

Aradia stood beside Lira, her wings shimmering with the light of victory. "You did it," she said softly, her eyes filled with respect. "You saved the forest."

Lira looked out over the clearing, her heart swelling with pride. "We did it. Together."

As the sun set over the restored Enchanted Forest, Lira realized something important. Magic was not just about power—it was about unity, about standing together in the face of fear. The lesson was clear: only when hearts and minds worked as one could true magic be unleashed.

And with that, the forest thrived once again, its heart beating strong, as the unicorn and the Fairy Queen stood side by side, guardians of a magic that would never fade.

# The Last Horn

In the heart of the ancient forest, where the trees grew taller than castles and the air shimmered with forgotten magic, there lived a unicorn known only as Thalion. His coat was no longer the pure white it once had been, having faded over centuries into the color of moonlit stone. His mane, once flowing and wild, now hung in silver strands like the threads of a bygone era. But his horn—still sharp and gleaming—remained as powerful and as mystical as ever.

Thalion had lived for many lifetimes, witnessing the rise and fall of empires, the birth of magic, and the slow decay of civilizations. In his younger days, he had been a symbol of purity and power, a creature of myth and legend. Now, he was the last of his kind, the only unicorn left to walk the earth, and he had come to the decision that it was time to share his stories.

Each week, a group of young creatures would gather around him in the clearing by the great oak tree. They were not all unicorns; many were griffins, phoenixes, and lesser-known magical beings who had come to seek his wisdom. They listened in rapt silence as Thalion spoke of the old times, of kingdoms that had risen in the blink of an eye, only to fall into dust just as quickly.

"They thought themselves invincible," Thalion would say, his voice deep and steady. "But they did not understand that true power does not come from strength or riches. It comes from understanding the delicate balance of all things."

The younger creatures were fascinated by his tales. They asked questions about the ancient cities he had seen, the wars fought over magic, the alliances and betrayals that shaped the course of history. Thalion answered patiently, always with a deep sadness in his eyes, as though each lesson he imparted carried the weight of a thousand lifetimes.

One afternoon, as the sun began to set and the sky was painted in hues of purple and gold, a young griffin named Kael raised his talon and spoke up. "Master Thalion," Kael said, his voice filled with youthful enthusiasm, "why didn't you ever try to stop the kingdoms from falling? You were so powerful, so wise. Why didn't you prevent the destruction?"

Thalion's gaze turned to the horizon, his eyes reflecting the wisdom of ages. For a long time, he said nothing. The young creatures waited, sensing that this was a question that would not be answered lightly.

"Many times I tried," Thalion replied softly. "I tried to warn them, to guide them, but they were always too blinded by their own desires. They thought that by conquering others, they could secure their place in the world. But they were wrong. And in the end, their own greed consumed them."

"But could you not have stopped it?" Kael pressed, his wings fluttering with excitement. "With your magic, surely you could have turned the tide. Stopped the wars, united the kingdoms."

Thalion turned his ancient eyes to the griffin, and there was a depth in his gaze that Kael had never seen before. "Power is not always about what one can do. It is about what one chooses not to do. I could have used my magic to force peace, to end the wars. But the moment I did that, I would have become just as blinded as those I sought to stop. The balance of the world is fragile, Kael. If I had imposed my will on them, I would have changed the course of history in ways that could never be undone. And sometimes, even when it hurts, it is better to allow things to fall as they must."

The creatures around the clearing fell silent, contemplating the weight of Thalion's words. Kael's youthful face contorted in confusion. "But isn't that the point? Isn't it the responsibility of those who can do something to make things right?"

Thalion's horn glowed faintly in the twilight, the magic within him stirring with the weight of the ages. "Responsibility is not just about acting. It is about knowing when to act, and when to step back. In my long life, I have seen that sometimes, the greatest wisdom lies in patience—waiting for the right moment to make a change. To act too hastily is to risk making things worse than they were."

"But everything you said—about the kingdoms and the wars—everything was lost," Kael argued, his young voice trembling with frustration. "You didn't do anything, and all those lives were lost."

Thalion's gaze softened, and he stepped closer to the griffin. "I did something," he said gently. "I lived. I watched. I learned. And I passed on what I learned to others, like you. Perhaps, in the future, you will be the one to make the change that is needed. But you must be patient. You must understand the consequences of your actions, the ripple effect they will have on everything around you."

Kael shook his head, unable to fully grasp the meaning behind Thalion's words. "But... how can we know what the right thing to do is?"

Thalion lowered his head, his horn now touching the earth. "The right thing to do, Kael, is not always clear. But it is not about knowing the answers—it is about asking the right questions. The answers will come in time, but only if you are willing to listen, to learn, and to grow."

The young creatures looked at one another, unsure of what to make of this cryptic advice. Kael's frustration was evident, but he also understood that there was more to this lesson than he could yet comprehend.

As the stars began to twinkle overhead, Thalion continued. "You are all young, and you are eager to change the world. But remember this: The world is never changed by force alone. It is changed by understanding, by compassion, and by the choices we make, one by one. And sometimes, the most powerful change comes from within, when we learn to let go of our need to control everything."

The night deepened, and the creatures slowly began to leave, each one carrying Thalion's words with them. Kael, however, remained seated, looking up at the ancient unicorn.

"I still don't understand," Kael admitted, his voice small.

Thalion smiled, his eyes twinkling with the light of a thousand untold stories. "And you may never fully understand, Kael. But that is the nature of wisdom. It is not something to be possessed—it is something to be experienced."

As the last of the young creatures disappeared into the shadows, Thalion stood alone, his gaze fixed on the vast, empty forest. He had lived through centuries of triumph and failure, and as the last of his kind, he knew that his time was coming to an end. But he had no regrets. For in the end, he had learned the most important lesson of all: That true power lies not in control, but in the willingness to understand the delicate balance of all things.

And with that, the ancient unicorn, the witness to a thousand lifetimes, walked silently into the night, knowing that the future was no longer his to shape. The young ones would carry on, and they would find their own path, just as he had once done.

# The Heart of the Hunt

Sir Edric was young, but he was determined. A knight of noble blood, he had been trained since childhood in the ways of combat, discipline, and duty. His swordsmanship was unparalleled, and his armor shone like polished silver under the sun. His family's legacy was built on valor, and he was expected to continue that tradition. So when the king himself had tasked him with capturing a unicorn—a rare and mystical creature that had eluded every hunter for centuries—Edric had not hesitated. It was a mission of glory, one that would bring him fame beyond measure.

The forest was dense and wild, a place where the air was thick with the scent of ancient trees and the rustle of unseen creatures. Edric had spent days tracking the unicorn's elusive hoofprints, each step feeling more like a challenge than the last. The deeper he ventured into the forest, the more the air seemed to hum with magic. There were whispers in the wind, strange and soft, but Edric dismissed them as nothing more than superstition.

The unicorn was a creature of legend, described as pure as moonlight, with a silver-white coat and a spiraling horn that glowed with the power of the ancient world. Its blood was said to have miraculous properties, capable of healing the gravest of wounds, bestowing strength beyond imagination. To capture it would mean not just glory but wealth, power, and favor from the king. And for a young knight like Edric, those things were all that mattered.

He had been warned, of course, by those who spoke in hushed voices at taverns and firesides. "The unicorn is not to be captured," they would say. "It is a creature of light, meant to roam free in the wilds. To hunt it is to destroy something that should never be touched by human hands." But Edric had scoffed at such words. The forest was a place of beauty, yes, but it was also a place of challenge. A knight's duty was to conquer, not to cower in fear of some myth.

For three days, Edric followed the trail. And then, on the fourth, he found it.

The unicorn stood in a clearing, bathed in the soft light of the setting sun. Its coat shimmered like woven silver, and its horn, like a twist of moonlight, seemed to pulse with an otherworldly energy. For a moment, Edric froze. He had expected awe, but what he felt instead was something far more profound—a deep sense of wonder, followed by an inexplicable sadness.

The unicorn looked at him, its large eyes filled with a knowing, unspoken understanding. It seemed to know the intent of the hunter before the first step was taken, yet it did not run. It merely stood there, calm and majestic, as if waiting.

Edric's hand moved instinctively to his sword. This was the moment. He had come so far, endured so much. His grip tightened on the hilt, and yet, as he stepped closer, something inside him shifted. His heart, once filled with the anticipation of victory, now ached with uncertainty. The creature was not like the beasts he had hunted before. It was pure, untouchable.

He hesitated.

For the first time in his life, Edric questioned what it meant to be a knight. Was his duty truly to take what he could conquer, to claim victory over all things, regardless of the cost? Or was there more to his calling—something greater than mere glory?

The unicorn did not move as Edric approached, and it was then that he saw something else: a deep wound on its side, as if it had been struck by a sharp object. Blood, dark and thick, stained the silver of its coat. A knot of guilt formed in Edric's stomach. Had the creature been injured by someone else? Someone like him? Had it already suffered, and yet it stood here, waiting for him to finish what had already begun?

The unicorn's eyes met his again, and in that moment, Edric felt a rush of emotions he could not explain. The sadness, the guilt, the overwhelming urge to protect this beautiful, innocent being. It was not the magic of the unicorn that had ensnared him, but its unspoken plea.

Edric lowered his sword, his heart racing. "I cannot do this," he whispered, as much to himself as to the creature before him. The call for glory, for fame, for riches—it all seemed hollow now. What was the point of victory when it came at the cost of something so pure, so irreplaceable?

The unicorn took a step toward him, its movements graceful and fluid. It nuzzled his hand gently, as if understanding his decision. For a brief moment, Edric felt a connection—a bond that transcended words, transcended the need to capture or control. It was a moment of profound understanding. The unicorn was not meant to be captured; it was meant to be revered, to be left in the wild where it could live in peace, untouched by the greed of men.

Edric stepped back, his mind made up. "I will not harm you," he said, his voice steady. "You are free."

As if sensing the sincerity in his words, the unicorn turned and, with a grace that seemed impossible for such a large creature, disappeared into the trees. Edric stood there for a long time, watching the place where it had vanished, the weight of his decision settling over him like a heavy cloak.

When he returned to the castle, empty-handed, the king was furious. "You failed," the king shouted, his voice echoing through the stone halls. "You were sent to capture the unicorn, not to let it escape!"

Edric did not flinch. "I did not fail, my lord," he replied, his voice calm. "I chose not to capture it. Some things are meant to be left in peace, and that is what I have done."

The king scoffed, dismissing him as foolish, a knight who had forgotten the true meaning of duty. But Edric stood firm, knowing that in that forest, he had discovered something far more important than any title or reward.

The days that followed were long and difficult for Edric. He was no longer the hero that returned with the prize, but a knight who had defied orders for the sake of a creature that represented something beyond his own ambitions. But in the silence of the castle, away from the praise and the glory, Edric felt a quiet sense of pride. He had learned a lesson that could never be taken from him: the greatest victories are not the ones we win through conquest, but the ones we earn through understanding and compassion.

# The Midnight Circle

The night of the full moon had always held an air of mystery in the enchanted valley of Thalor. The villagers whispered about it in their homes, casting wary glances toward the woods when the moonlight bathed the land in an eerie glow. The trees themselves seemed to hum with anticipation, their ancient branches creaking under the weight of something unspoken. On this particular night, the air felt different—a subtle, electric charge that vibrated through the forest, causing even the most steadfast creatures to pause. It was the night when the unicorns would gather.

Rian, a young woman of the village, had heard the stories for as long as she could remember. Her grandmother had spoken of the unicorns with reverence, telling her tales of their beauty, grace, and the powerful magic they wielded. But she had never seen them herself—no one had. The unicorns, it was said, only appeared on the night of the full moon, when the world itself seemed to hold its breath in reverence. On that night, they performed a ritual, something ancient and powerful, deep in the heart of the hidden meadow.

Rian had always been curious. The pull to witness this secret gathering had grown stronger as the years passed, her desire to understand the true nature of these mythical creatures consuming her thoughts. On this particular night, however, her curiosity was stronger than ever. The full moon hung low in the sky, its pale light casting long shadows across the valley, and Rian made her decision. She would see the unicorns tonight, no matter what.

With quiet determination, she slipped from her home and into the woods, careful not to disturb the natural silence of the night. The forest was alive in its own way, with creatures scurrying in the underbrush, their eyes catching the light in strange flashes. Rian's heart raced as she followed the winding path she had memorized over the years, leading to the meadow that had been kept secret from the world. She had heard that only those pure of heart could find their way to the gathering. She hoped that her yearning for truth was enough to guide her.

After what seemed like an eternity of walking, the trees began to thin, and she found herself standing at the edge of the meadow. The air here was different—warmer, charged with a sense of ancient power. The grass shimmered under the moonlight, and in the center of the meadow, a circle of unicorns had gathered. Their coats glistened like starlight, their long, twisting horns gleaming as if they held the very essence of the cosmos within them. The scene was breathtaking, the kind of beauty that stopped the heart and made the world feel impossibly small.

Rian watched in awe from the shadows, not daring to move, as the unicorns stood in a circle. Their eyes were closed, their movements slow and deliberate. With every step they took, the air seemed to shimmer more brightly, and Rian could feel the magic of the ritual rising around her. She could hear a low, melodic hum in the air, as if the earth itself was singing along with the creatures. This was not a gathering of beasts; it was a communion, an ancient bond that had lasted long before any human had walked the earth.

The unicorns' leader, a majestic silver-coated mare whose horn spiraled with delicate threads of gold, stepped into the center of the circle. She raised her head high, and the ground beneath her hooves trembled. Rian watched, fascinated, as the mare closed her eyes and began to chant in a language that was both foreign and familiar, like a memory that could not quite be recalled. The words seemed to vibrate in the air, stirring something deep inside Rian's chest.

As the chant grew louder, the moon above them seemed to respond. Its light intensified, casting beams that turned the meadow into a sea of shimmering silver. The unicorns began to move in perfect synchrony, their hooves leaving trails of stardust in the air as they circled the mare. Rian could feel her pulse quicken, the magic of the ritual surging around her, and for a moment, she thought she might lose herself in it.

But then, as the chanting reached a crescendo, something unexpected happened. One of the unicorns, a dark-coated stallion with piercing blue eyes, turned his head towards Rian. His gaze locked onto hers, and for a moment, time seemed to stop. The unicorn's eyes were not just eyes—they were a window into something far greater. Rian felt herself drawn into them, as if the very essence of the creature was pulling her in, connecting her to something beyond her understanding.

Her breath caught in her throat. She knew then that the unicorns were not just magical creatures—they were ancient beings, protectors of the land and the balance of the world. And she was standing in the middle of their most sacred moment.

The stallion's eyes softened, and for a brief moment, Rian thought she saw a flicker of sadness. As if understanding her confusion, he took a step forward, breaking the circle. The ritual faltered for a heartbeat as the others paused, but then the mare's voice rang out, cutting through the tension.

"No," she said, her voice a melody that seemed to soothe the dissonance in the air. "It is time."

Rian's heart pounded in her chest as the stallion approached her. His steps were slow, deliberate. He stopped in front of her, his gaze never leaving hers. "You have come to witness the ritual," he said, his voice not one of words but of thought—an unspoken communication that resonated in her very being. "But the truth you seek is not in what you see tonight."

Rian's voice trembled as she spoke, unsure of the words forming in her mind. "What is it, then? What is the ritual? Why are you gathering here?"

The stallion's horn glowed faintly, and the air around them seemed to hum. "This is not a ritual of magic," he explained. "It is a ritual of remembrance. The unicorns are not just creatures of power—they are the keepers of balance, the guardians of the ancient ways. But we have forgotten, just as humanity has forgotten the old ways. We gather not to harness magic, but to restore it. To remind ourselves of what we are."

Rian's mind reeled with the weight of the words. The unicorns, it seemed, had not come to the world to be worshipped or captured, but to remind it of something vital—something lost. They were the keepers of something far older than magic, something essential to the very fabric of life itself.

As the ritual concluded, the unicorns slowly began to fade into the shadows, their figures melting into the night. The mare nodded once more at Rian, and as she turned to follow her kin, she whispered, "The world is not what it seems. Seek the truth beyond what is visible. That is the real magic."

Rian stood in the meadow long after the unicorns had gone, the silence thick around her. The moonlight no longer shimmered as it had before. It was as if the very air had shifted, the world holding its breath in the wake of something profound. She had come seeking magic, but what she had found was something more—something that would change her life forever.

As the last of the unicorns vanished into the night, Rian realized that the ritual had not been for them. It had been for her.

# The Horn of Truth

In the heart of the ancient forest, where the trees whispered secrets older than time itself, there was a unicorn unlike any other. Her name was Nyssa, and she had lived for centuries, guarding the magic of the forest and maintaining the balance between the known world and the unseen. Nyssa's horn was as pure as the moonlight that bathed the forest, a spiral of crystal that shimmered with the power to reveal the truth of anyone it touched. No lie, no deception, could withstand its touch. The Horn of Truth, as it was known, was the forest's most sacred treasure—protected fiercely, its power respected by all who walked the land.

One autumn evening, a stranger came to the forest. His name was Alistair, a man with a smooth voice and a charming smile that made others believe he was trustworthy. He had traveled far, his clothes worn from the journey, his eyes clouded with secrets. He had heard the legends of the unicorn and the Horn of Truth, and he had come with a singular purpose: to use it.

Alistair found Nyssa at the edge of a moonlit clearing, her silver coat glowing softly in the pale light. She was grazing, calm and serene, but the moment he stepped into the clearing, her head snapped up, her eyes meeting his. She knew the moment he arrived. She always did.

"You seek something, stranger," Nyssa's voice was like the rustling of leaves, soft yet powerful. "What is it you want from me?"

Alistair took a step forward, his confidence unwavering. "I have come to seek the truth. I've heard of your power, your ability to reveal what lies beneath the surface. I am ready to face it."

Nyssa regarded him carefully. She had seen many come before him—many who sought the truth for their own gain, their own desires. But something about Alistair felt different, as if his words were more than just the usual plea for knowledge. There was a darkness in his eyes that she could not ignore.

"The truth is not something to be taken lightly," Nyssa warned. "It has a power of its own, one that can unravel more than you are prepared to lose. Are you truly ready to face it?"

Alistair nodded, his expression unwavering. "I am. I have nothing left to lose."

Nyssa's eyes narrowed. She sensed the lie in his words, but she said nothing. The Horn of Truth had its own way of revealing what was hidden. She stepped closer, her horn glowing softly, and with a gentle movement, she touched it to Alistair's hand.

The moment the horn made contact with his skin, a strange energy filled the air. The forest seemed to hold its breath. For a brief second, everything was still. And then, without warning, the world around them began to twist. The trees shifted unnaturally, their branches stretching and bending in impossible ways. The moonlight flickered, like a candle caught in the wind, casting strange, distorted shadows across the ground. Alistair gasped, his body trembling as though the very earth beneath him had come alive.

"What is happening?" Alistair cried out, his voice tinged with panic.

Nyssa stepped back, watching him with a detached calmness. The Horn of Truth had never behaved in such a way before. The lies he carried with him were not merely words. They were deep, insidious, and the horn was struggling to unravel them, to expose them for what they were. It was as if Alistair's very existence was built on a foundation of deceit.

Alistair staggered, his knees buckling as he fell to the ground. The twisted vision around him grew more intense, the shadows elongating and swallowing the light. He clutched his head, trying to make sense of the chaos that surrounded him.

"You have lied to more than just me, haven't you?" Nyssa's voice cut through the disorienting noise. "Your lies are not simply to protect yourself. They are to hide the truth from those who need it most. But the truth cannot be buried forever."

Alistair looked up at her, his eyes wide with fear and desperation. "I—I don't know what you mean. I haven't done anything wrong."

But the moment he spoke, the world around him fractured again. The forest blurred, and a vision appeared before him—a memory, or perhaps a dream. He saw a woman, her face twisted in anguish, her hands reaching out to him. A child, lying lifeless on the ground, surrounded by blood. And Alistair, standing over her, his face cold, his hands stained with something more than just regret.

The truth was no longer a distant thing. It was here, in front of him, demanding to be acknowledged. Alistair's breath caught in his throat as the memory played out in vivid detail. He saw his own betrayal, his lies, the false promises he had made to cover his tracks, to escape the consequences of his actions. He had told the world one story, but the truth had been something entirely different.

The world began to settle, the twisted vision receding, but the pain remained. Alistair's body trembled, his heart pounding with a sense of horror he had never felt before. The weight of his lies had caught up to him, and it was a burden he could no longer ignore.

Nyssa stood over him, her horn still glowing, the power of truth lingering in the air like a heavy fog. "The truth will always find its way to the surface," she said quietly. "You can lie to others, even to yourself, but it will not change what is real. You have to live with the consequences of your choices, Alistair."

Alistair could barely lift his head, the shame of his actions bearing down on him. The truth, which he had tried so desperately to avoid, had been laid bare before him. And now, there was nothing left to hide behind.

"Why did you let me do this?" he whispered, his voice breaking. "Why didn't you stop me?"

Nyssa's eyes softened, though her expression remained firm. "Because you needed to see it for yourself. The truth cannot be forced upon anyone. It must be embraced willingly. Only then can it heal."

For a long time, Alistair sat there, the weight of the moment pressing down on him. The world around him had returned to its natural state, the trees standing tall, the moonlight once again soft and serene. But for him, nothing would ever be the same. The lies that had shaped his life, the ones he had told others and the ones he had told himself, had crumbled in an instant. He was no longer the man who had come seeking the truth. He was someone new, someone who had to face the consequences of his own actions.

As he rose to his feet, Nyssa stepped back, watching him with a quiet understanding. "The truth is not a weapon," she said softly. "It is a guide. It will lead you to redemption, but only if you are willing to walk the path."

Alistair nodded, though his heart felt heavy. The truth had stripped him of his illusions, and now he was left to rebuild himself, piece by piece. But as he looked into Nyssa's eyes, he realized that, in the end, the pain of facing the truth was far less than the torment of living in its shadow.

And for the first time in his life, Alistair understood.

# The Last Gift

The village of Lorian sat at the edge of the Mistwood, a dark and mysterious forest where the trees seemed to stretch endlessly toward the sky, their thick branches woven together like a canopy of secrets. For generations, the villagers had lived in harmony with the forest, knowing that magic thrived just beyond their borders. However, this peace was shattered when a strange illness began to spread through the village, claiming the lives of the young and old alike. It came without warning—swift and silent—and none could find a cure.

The village healer, an old woman named Elara, had done everything she could. Potions, herbs, rituals—nothing worked. The illness had no name, and no one knew how to stop it. The village was desperate, their spirits growing darker with each passing day.

On the third week of the outbreak, a mysterious figure appeared at the edge of the village just as the moon was rising. It was a unicorn—its coat shimmering silver under the light of the moon, and its long, spiraling horn glowing with an otherworldly light. The villagers had heard of unicorns in the old tales, but they had never seen one before. The creature stood at the edge of the forest, its eyes calm and wise, as though it had waited for this moment.

Elara, though weakened by her own despair, was the first to approach. She knew of the unicorns—how they had once roamed freely, offering their gifts to those in need. But she also knew the price that came with such magic. The unicorn's powers were great, but they were never without consequence.

The unicorn stepped forward, its hooves light on the earth, and lowered its head. Elara hesitated but then knelt, placing a trembling hand on the unicorn's soft coat. She had heard the stories, but she had never truly believed. Now, in the presence of this creature, she felt both awe and fear.

"I can help," the unicorn said, its voice like a soft breeze, carrying the weight of centuries. "I can heal your people."

Elara swallowed hard, knowing that such a gift would not come without sacrifice. "What is the cost?" she asked, her voice barely a whisper.

The unicorn's eyes, deep and ancient, met hers. "The gift of life can only be exchanged for something equally precious. I can save your village, but I will take from you in return."

Elara's heart raced. "What do you mean? What must I give?"

The unicorn did not speak, but instead lowered its head, its horn glowing brightly. Elara could feel the power in the air, a crackling energy that seemed to hum through her very bones. She closed her eyes, knowing that this was a decision that would change everything.

"I will save them," the unicorn said. "But I will take from you the one thing that has always given you strength—your ability to love."

Elara gasped, her eyes flying open. "What? You would take my love?"

The unicorn nodded. "You will still care for your people, but the bond you feel, the warmth of your heart toward them—this will be gone. You will be a healer, but you will never again feel the deep connection that comes with your love. This is the price of my gift."

Elara's mind whirled. Could she sacrifice her ability to love for the sake of saving her people? She had spent her life caring for others, her heart bound to the village and its people. But they were dying—her friends, her neighbors, her family. She could not let them perish.

Tears filled her eyes as she gazed at the unicorn. "Do it," she whispered. "Save them."

The unicorn's horn glowed brightly, and the air seemed to vibrate with the pulse of magic. Elara felt a strange sensation, as though her very soul was being peeled back, stripped of the emotions she had carried for a lifetime. The warmth she had felt for the village, the love for her people, began to fade, leaving her hollow. It wasn't painful, but it was deeply unsettling—like waking from a dream that was too real to forget.

The unicorn's magic spread across the village like a wave, touching each person, healing them. The illness lifted, replaced by a sense of calm and peace that settled over the land. The villagers woke from their fevered slumbers, their bodies whole again, their spirits no longer weighed down by the sickness.

But when Elara looked into their eyes, something was different. They were well, yes, but there was no warmth in their gazes, no recognition of the love that had once been shared. It was as though they were strangers, as if the bond between them had been severed. She could no longer feel the connection that had once made her care so deeply for them.

The unicorn stepped back, its work complete. "The cost has been paid," it said softly, its voice laced with sadness. "You saved them, but now you must walk alone."

Elara stood in the center of the village, surrounded by those she had healed but no longer recognized. Her heart felt empty, as though the very essence of who she was had been taken from her. She had saved the village, but in doing so, she had lost herself.

As the unicorn turned to leave, Elara felt a sharp pang of longing—longing for the warmth she had given up, for the connection that had defined her life. She had saved her people, but she had done so at the cost of the one thing that made her human.

"Is this the price of magic?" she asked, her voice hoarse.

The unicorn did not turn back but spoke softly, as if understanding the depth of her sorrow. "Magic is not just power, Elara. It is balance. Every gift has its shadow, and every sacrifice leaves a mark. You have chosen to give your heart for the greater good. And in time, you will understand that love is not always the answer. Sometimes, survival is."

With those final words, the unicorn faded into the mist of the forest, leaving Elara standing in the village she had saved, but at what cost?

As the days passed, Elara continued her work as a healer. The village flourished, free from the illness that had threatened to tear them apart. But in her solitude, she began to understand the true nature of sacrifice. She could heal their bodies, but she could no longer heal their hearts—nor her own.

And so, Elara walked through her days, a healer without love, a woman who had saved a village but lost herself in the process. She had given everything to ensure their survival, but the emptiness within her grew, a silent reminder that not all gifts come without consequences. The village had been saved, but at the cost of something deeper, something irreplaceable. The gift of love, once given freely, was now a distant memory—lost in the shadow of the Horn of Truth.

# Whispers of the Last Leaf

Deep in the heart of the enchanted land, where the rivers whispered secrets and the trees held memories of forgotten centuries, there lived a unicorn named Elyra. Her forest, the Enchanted Wood, was her home, her sanctuary, and the source of her magic. The forest had thrived for eons, its every leaf and root imbued with the essence of life, protected by the unicorn's enduring magic. The trees towered high, their leaves shimmering with the light of the stars, and the flowers bloomed in colors unseen by the human eye. It was a place of beauty, where time seemed to stand still, and the air was thick with the hum of ancient power.

But lately, Elyra had felt a change in the air—a subtle shift that she couldn't ignore. The leaves no longer sparkled as they once had, and the rivers no longer sang with joy. The magic of the forest, her magic, was beginning to fade. Every day, more and more trees wilted, their vibrant colors turning dull, their branches bending under the weight of an unseen sorrow. The flowers withered at their roots, and the once-lush undergrowth turned dry and brittle. Elyra could feel the life force of the forest slipping away, and no matter how much she tried to call upon her magic, it was becoming harder to hold onto.

The unicorn stood at the edge of the forest, looking out over the land she had protected for centuries. Her heart ached as she watched the decay spread. The Enchanted Wood was dying, and she didn't know how to stop it. Elyra had always believed that the forest's magic was tied to her own, but now, even with all her power, she could feel the pull of something darker. The forest was not just fading—it was being drained of life, as if something was slowly consuming it from the inside.

Determined to find the cause, Elyra ventured deeper into the heart of the Enchanted Wood. The once-familiar paths now felt alien to her, the trees now more twisted and dark. There was no singing in the wind, no warmth in the sunlight. It was as though the very essence of the forest had been stolen. She wandered for hours, searching for any sign of what was causing the decay, but all she found was more destruction.

As the moon rose high in the sky, casting a pale light across the forest, Elyra stumbled upon a clearing she had not visited in centuries. In the center of the clearing stood an ancient tree, its bark twisted and gnarled, its branches reaching up to the sky like skeletal hands. This tree had once been the heart of the forest—the source of its magic. Elyra could feel its power pulsing faintly, but it was weak, dying, just like everything else around her.

And then she saw it—the source of the darkness. A shadow, dark as night, wrapped around the roots of the ancient tree, sucking the life out of it. The shadow seemed to writhe and pulse with a malevolent energy, and Elyra could feel the coldness radiating from it, a coldness that chilled her to the bone.

The unicorn approached cautiously, her horn glowing with a soft light. She called upon her magic, hoping to push back the shadow, but it resisted. The more she tried, the more the shadow seemed to grow, feeding off the forest's life force, its magic. Elyra's heart pounded in her chest as she realized the truth—this wasn't just a natural death. The forest was being killed, drained by something ancient and powerful. But what? And why?

The shadow seemed to sense her presence, shifting and swirling, forming into a shape—a figure cloaked in darkness, its face hidden from view. Elyra stepped back, her magic flaring with power, but the figure remained calm, its voice echoing in her mind.

"You cannot stop me, Elyra," the figure whispered, its voice like the rustle of dry leaves. "I am the consequence of the forest's own nature—the price it must pay for existing as it does."

Elyra's heart skipped a beat. "What do you mean? Why are you doing this? The forest has been your protector for centuries. It has given you everything."

The figure laughed, a sound that echoed like the cracking of branches in a storm. "The forest has always been a place of balance, Elyra. But balance does not last forever. The magic it holds must be reclaimed, consumed by what is natural. The forest's immortality is an illusion, a lie that you have fed to yourself for centuries. And now, the time has come for it to end."

The unicorn's horn glowed brighter, but it did not seem to affect the shadow. "I will not let you destroy it," Elyra said, her voice fierce.

The figure's form began to change, shifting into something darker, something older than even Elyra's magic. "You cannot stop the cycle," it said softly. "The forest must die, just as you must eventually die. The gift you have been given is not forever. The truth of your magic is that it is tied to the forest's life, and when it fades, so do you. You cannot hold on to the world forever, Elyra."

A chill ran through Elyra's body as the truth of the figure's words settled in. She had always believed that her magic was bound to the forest, but in reality, her power was only borrowed. She was the forest's guardian, but in the end, she too was subject to the cycle of life and death. Her magic, as powerful as it was, could not stop the inevitable.

Elyra fell to her knees, tears stinging her eyes as the full weight of the realization hit her. The forest had given her a gift—a gift of immortality and power—but it was not hers to keep. She had been living on borrowed time, and now the time had come for the forest to die, for the cycle to begin anew.

But as she knelt there, a new thought arose in her mind. The forest may have been dying, but that didn't mean its magic had to disappear. Elyra understood now that the forest's essence was not just in its trees, its rivers, or its creatures. The magic of the forest was in its balance, its cycles of life and death, and in the hearts of those who protected it. Perhaps the shadow was right—the forest could not live forever. But it didn't have to be destroyed. It could be reborn.

With a final surge of power, Elyra reached out to the dying tree, her horn glowing brighter than it ever had before. She channeled all her magic, her energy, and her love for the forest into the roots of the ancient tree. She let go of the fear, the sorrow, and the belief that her magic was the only thing keeping the forest alive. She understood now that the forest, like all things, must change and evolve.

The shadow screamed as it was consumed by the light, and Elyra felt the forest's heartbeat slow. The trees began to sway, their leaves rustling in a soft breeze. The darkness receded, and in its place, a new energy filled the air—one of renewal, of hope. The forest would not die; it would transform, adapt, and continue.

Elyra rose to her feet, her heart lighter than it had been in centuries. The forest was not immortal, but it was resilient. And she, too, would change. The magic of the forest had never been hers alone. It had always belonged to the land, to the balance of life and death.

And in that moment, Elyra understood: true power comes not from holding on, but from knowing when to let go. The forest would thrive again, and so would she.

# The Stolen Horn

Lira was young, but her horn was unlike any other in the enchanted valley where she lived. It was long and gleaming, with swirling patterns that seemed to shimmer and pulse with the magic of the ancient world. It was the source of her strength, her ability to heal, and her connection to the world around her. The unicorns of her herd had always told her that the horn was a gift—a part of her, a symbol of the natural harmony that existed between herself and the land.

One morning, Lira woke to find the impossible had occurred—her horn was gone. The place where it had once rested, shining with radiant light, was now empty. Panic surged through her, and she ran through the meadow calling for the others, but her cries went unanswered. Her herd had vanished. There was no trace of them, no sign of struggle or disturbance. It was as if the entire world had quietly turned its back on her.

In the midst of her despair, Lira noticed a faint trail leading away from the meadow—a set of small footprints, too delicate to belong to any creature of the forest, but unmistakably human. Her heart pounded. She could not fathom why someone would want her horn, but she knew she had no choice but to follow the trail. The magic of her people, the connection they shared with the land, had been stolen from her. If she did not get it back, the balance would begin to unravel.

Lira followed the trail for days, crossing rivers and climbing hills, but the thief was always one step ahead. Her body, though swift and graceful, began to tire, her magic weakened with each passing hour. She could feel the forest around her responding to her growing sense of fear and desperation. The once-vibrant land seemed muted, as if the life force had been drained from it, just as her own strength had been. She could feel her connection to the earth slipping away.

It wasn't until the third night of her journey, beneath a sky crowded with stars, that she reached the outskirts of a small village. The buildings were low and made of rough-hewn stone, nestled in a valley far from the reach of the enchanted forest. The air felt different here—thicker, tainted by something unnatural. Lira approached cautiously, hiding in the shadows, trying to make sense of what she saw. In the center of the village square stood a man—tall, dressed in dark robes, and holding something aloft in his hands. Her heart stopped. It was her horn.

Lira's breath caught in her throat as she watched the man stand in the middle of the square, the stolen horn glowing in his hands. He wasn't just holding it—he was using it. The air around him twisted, and with every wave of the horn, the ground seemed to crack and shift. The village was changing, the magic corrupting everything in its path. Trees withered, the earth cracked open, and the animals fled in terror. This was no ordinary thief. This man, this dark sorcerer, had stolen not just her horn but the life force of the land itself.

Without hesitation, Lira charged into the square, her hooves pounding against the cobblestones, the air crackling with the last remnants of her magic. The sorcerer turned slowly, a wicked grin spreading across his face as he recognized her.

"So, the little unicorn finally catches up to me," the sorcerer sneered. "You have no idea how powerful this horn is, do you? How much potential it holds. I've spent years searching for it, waiting for the right moment to claim it."

Lira's voice trembled with a mix of anger and desperation. "Why? Why would you steal it? The horn is a gift—my gift to the land. Without it, everything will die."

The sorcerer laughed, a hollow sound that echoed through the desolate village. "You fool. The land? The forest? It's all an illusion. The true power lies in what I can do with this horn. With it, I can control everything—bend the very earth to my will. And you... you are nothing more than a tool, a means to an end."

Lira's eyes burned with fury as she charged at the sorcerer, but before she could reach him, he raised the horn high, and a blinding light shot from its tip, knocking her back. She lay sprawled on the cobblestones, gasping for breath, her body aching from the impact. The sorcerer stood over her, his grin widening as he held the horn to his chest.

"You've always been too naïve to understand, unicorn," he taunted. "Your people were just as foolish. Protecting the land, guarding magic that was meant to be harnessed. But now, I will show you what true power looks like."

But as the sorcerer spoke, something unexpected began to happen. The ground beneath him started to rumble, the earth groaning as if in protest. The horn, once glowing with a vibrant light, began to flicker and dim. Lira, still weak but determined, watched as the sorcerer's face twisted in confusion.

"What's happening?" the sorcerer shouted, his voice now tinged with panic. "This isn't supposed to happen! The power should be mine!"

The horn began to glow again, but now its light was pulsing wildly, no longer under the sorcerer's control. Lira, despite her pain, realized what had gone wrong. The horn had never belonged to him. It was a conduit, yes, but it was always meant to connect with the land, with the unicorns who cared for it. It was a symbiotic bond—one that could not be broken without consequences. The horn was not just an instrument of power; it was the heart of the forest, and it rejected the sorcerer's attempts to control it.

With a final, desperate cry, the sorcerer dropped the horn as it pulsed with wild energy. He stumbled backward, his form twisting as the magic he sought to control turned on him. The light of the horn flared, and the earth beneath him opened up, swallowing him whole.

Lira, still lying on the ground, watched as the sorcerer vanished, consumed by his own greed. The horn fell gently beside her, its glow now calm and steady. Slowly, with great effort, she lifted herself and nudged the horn with her nose. The land, she could feel, was healing. The trees began to grow once more, the flowers bloomed, and the rivers flowed again.

But as she stood, she realized something important—she hadn't just recovered her horn. She had learned something she had never truly understood before. The horn, the power it held, wasn't just for one person or one creature. It was a part of something much larger than herself. The true magic was in the connection, in the sharing, not the taking.

As she returned to her forest, now alive and thriving once more, Lira understood that the balance of the world was fragile. Power, when hoarded, destroyed. But when shared, when allowed to flow freely, it could heal. The lesson she had learned was one she would carry with her for the rest of her life. True power lies not in control, but in connection.

# A Dream of Unicorns

Every night, as the moonlight filtered through the curtains of her room, Lily drifted into a world she could never fully understand—a world filled with unicorns. The first time it happened, she had woken up in the middle of the night with the vivid image of a unicorn's silvery mane shimmering in her mind, but as time passed, the dreams became more frequent, more intense, as though the creatures were reaching out to her, inviting her into their world.

The dreams were always the same: a sprawling meadow bathed in a soft, otherworldly glow. The air smelled of fresh grass and something ancient, like a forgotten secret waiting to be uncovered. The unicorns, with their coats as white as snow and their horns gleaming with iridescent light, would stand in a circle around her, their eyes full of wisdom and kindness. The dreams felt real, almost more real than her waking life, and when she awoke in the morning, she would feel a lingering warmth, as though the magic of the dream still pulsed through her veins.

At first, Lily thought little of it. Dreams were just dreams, after all, fleeting things that came and went with no true meaning. But the more it happened, the more she began to question what was real and what wasn't. One evening, after yet another vivid dream where the unicorns had surrounded her with their soft, knowing gazes, Lily awoke to find something strange: her pillow was wet, damp with tears she had not shed while asleep.

"Maybe I'm just tired," she muttered, wiping her face as she looked at the clock. It was the early hours of the morning, and her body was still heavy with sleep. But as she rolled over to bury her face in the pillow, she froze.

There, beneath the fabric, something sparkled—a soft, glowing light that shimmered beneath the pillow. Her heart raced, and she pulled the pillow away, revealing a small crystal, shaped like a star. It glowed with a soft, pulsing light, almost as though it was alive. She held it up, her breath catching in her throat. It was unlike anything she had ever seen before, and as she ran her fingers along its smooth surface, she felt a strange warmth radiating from it, as though the crystal was connected to something far beyond the material world.

The next night, the dream came again. The meadow, the unicorns, the soft glow of the moon. But this time, something was different. As she stood in the middle of the circle of unicorns, the leader of the herd, a majestic unicorn with a horn that glittered like the stars themselves, stepped forward. Its eyes locked onto hers, and Lily felt a pull in her chest, an undeniable connection that seemed to resonate deep within her soul.

"You have come to us," the unicorn spoke, its voice like a distant melody. "The crystal you hold is the key to a world hidden from your eyes, a world that exists just beyond your reach."

Lily blinked, her heart racing. "The crystal? What does it mean?"

The unicorn lowered its head, its horn glowing brighter. "The crystal is a gift—a bond between our world and yours. You are the chosen one, the one who will bridge the gap between the realms and bring balance to both. The magic within you has always been there, dormant, waiting to be awakened."

Lily could hardly believe what she was hearing. "But I'm just... me. I'm no one special. How can I possibly help?"

The unicorn's eyes softened with an ancient wisdom. "You are more than you know, Lily. The magic of the unicorns flows through you, through all who are open to it. The dreams you have are not mere fantasies. They are glimpses into the true nature of the world, and you have been chosen to see it, to understand it."

As the unicorn spoke, the other unicorns gathered around her, their eyes glowing with the same soft light as the crystal in her hand. The meadow seemed to pulse with energy, and Lily felt her heart synchronize with the rhythm of the world. She closed her eyes, and when she opened them again, the dream was no longer just a dream. It was a reality—a reality that she could touch, that she could feel.

"Come," the unicorn said, beckoning her forward. "Follow us, and you will see."

Lily stepped forward, and in the blink of an eye, she was no longer in the meadow. She stood in a place that defied understanding—a forest made of light and shadows, where the trees were alive with whispers, and the air crackled with magic. The world felt alive, as though every leaf, every stone, every drop of water had a story to tell, and it was waiting for her to listen.

The unicorns walked ahead of her, their hooves making no sound as they moved through the ethereal forest. Lily followed, her mind racing with questions, her heart filled with wonder. She had always felt disconnected from the world around her, as if there was something she couldn't grasp, something just beyond her reach. Now, here in this magical realm, everything felt whole, everything made sense.

They reached a clearing, and at its center was a pool of water, its surface perfectly still. The unicorns gathered around it, and the leader turned to Lily.

"Look into the water," it said, its voice a soft whisper in the wind.

Lily knelt beside the pool, her reflection staring back at her. But as she looked deeper, the reflection began to change. Her image shifted, becoming more radiant, more powerful, as though the very essence of magic was flowing through her. The image of the unicorns in the water rippled, blending with her reflection, becoming one.

"You are the link," the unicorn said. "You are the bridge between worlds, the keeper of balance. But the question remains: Will you stay here, with us, in this world of magic, or will you return to yours, bringing the magic with you?"

Lily's heart ached. She had never felt more at home than she did here, surrounded by the unicorns, in a world that was pure and untouched. But there was still her life in the waking world—her friends, her family, her responsibilities. She could feel the weight of the decision pressing on her.

"You are the keeper of both worlds," the unicorn said, as if reading her thoughts. "And the magic will follow you, no matter where you go. But remember this: to truly see, you must open your heart to both the wonder and the pain of the world. Magic is not just a gift. It is a responsibility."

Lily stood, feeling the weight of the crystal in her pocket, now alive with its own warmth. She looked at the unicorns one last time, then turned her gaze back to the pool. She could see the path ahead of her, a path that would require balance, a path that would ask her to carry the magic within her into a world that might not yet understand it.

When Lily awoke the next morning, she held the crystal in her hand, its glow still soft and steady. She knew now that the dream was more than just a dream. The magic was real, and so was the responsibility. The unicorns had given her a gift, but it was one she would have to carry for the rest of her life.

And as she stepped into the day, Lily understood. The magic was not in the world she had left behind, nor in the world she had entered. It was within her, always. The bridge between the realms was not a place—it was a journey.

# The Tides of Fire and Light

Once, the unicorns and the dragons were bitter enemies, their hatred as old as the first dawn. The dragons, with their fiery breath and towering strength, roamed the skies and the mountain peaks, while the unicorns, with their pure magic and ethereal grace, roamed the forests and meadows. For centuries, they fought—battles waged across the heavens and the earth—each side determined to claim dominion over the land. The dragons wanted to conquer the world with their power, while the unicorns sought to protect its delicate balance. It was a conflict that seemed endless, and it had left both sides scarred.

But that was before the Shadow came.

At first, it was nothing more than a whisper on the wind, a darkening of the skies. It started in the deep forests, where no one ventured, and spread slowly, quietly, like a disease. It took shape in the form of creatures—monsters of shadow and darkness that ravaged everything in their path. The land trembled with their hunger, and no magic, no fire, could stop them. Entire villages were swallowed by the darkness, their people lost to the void.

Both dragons and unicorns had tried to fight the Shadow alone. But they had failed. Their powers, though great, were no match for the darkness that consumed everything. The Shadow was not a creature, not a force of nature. It was a presence—an absence—a void that devoured light and life alike.

And so, in a moment of desperate realization, the leaders of the unicorns and the dragons convened. What was left of their pride and hatred fell away in the face of the greater threat. They had no choice but to work together.

Kael, a young dragon whose scales gleamed like molten gold, stood at the meeting of the two armies. His heart burned with the memory of the battles fought and the blood shed between his kin and the unicorns. But he knew, as did every other dragon present, that they could not defeat the Shadow alone. He stood beside his lifelong enemy, Arwen, a regal unicorn with a mane that shone like silver and a horn that shimmered with ancient magic. She was the embodiment of grace, her very presence a reminder of the purity and strength the unicorns had always held. They locked eyes, their past animosities nothing more than distant memories in the face of the present threat.

"We must join forces," Arwen said, her voice calm but filled with determination. "Our powers alone cannot banish the Shadow. We must unite if we are to have any chance."

Kael's gaze flickered toward the battlefield ahead, where the first of the Shadow's monsters began to emerge from the darkness. "You know I don't trust you, unicorn," he growled, the rumble in his chest sending a slight tremor through the air. "But if there's any chance of stopping this, we have no choice."

Arwen nodded, acknowledging the truth of his words. "We can put aside our past for the future. Let the strength of the dragon and the purity of the unicorn work together to defeat the true enemy."

And so, they did.

The dragons and unicorns fought side by side, their magic and strength intertwining in ways that neither had ever imagined. The dragons breathed fire, their flames illuminating the darkness, while the unicorns called upon their magic, weaving shields of light and healing the wounded. It was a fierce battle, unlike any they had fought before. The monsters of the Shadow were relentless, but the combined might of fire and light began to push them back.

But the Shadow itself was a clever thing. As the battle raged on, Kael and Arwen found themselves standing at the heart of the conflict, facing the largest of the creatures—the source of the Shadow's power. Its eyes burned with the darkness of a thousand nightmares, and it towered over them like a mountain made of shadows and fear.

Kael stepped forward, his wings flaring, his claws ready for the final strike. But Arwen stopped him with a gentle hoof. "It's not the creature we must fight," she said, her voice quiet but certain. "It is the Shadow itself."

Kael looked at her, confused. "What are you talking about?"

"The Shadow feeds on fear and hatred," Arwen explained, her horn glowing with a soft, ethereal light. "It is not a monster to be slain with force. It is an absence, a lack of light and love. To defeat it, we must fill the emptiness with something stronger—something that cannot be consumed."

Kael's eyes narrowed, understanding dawning on him. He had always believed that strength alone could overcome any enemy. But now, in the face of this dark force, he saw the truth in Arwen's words. The Shadow could not be defeated by power alone. They had to unite, not just in body, but in spirit.

Kael hesitated, then lowered his head in reluctant acceptance. "What do you suggest?"

Arwen closed her eyes, calling upon the magic of her people, summoning the light within her. Kael, though uncertain, did the same, letting the fire inside him burn brighter than ever. As their magic intertwined, something unexpected happened. The ground beneath them began to glow, the light spreading outward in a wave, pushing back the darkness.

For a moment, nothing happened. The Shadow seemed to resist, pushing against the light as though it would consume it. But then, slowly, the light grew stronger, and the darkness began to recede. The creatures of the Shadow shrieked and crumbled, their forms dissolving into nothingness. And at the center of it all, the Shadow itself began to vanish, its power fading like a dying ember.

The battle was over. The Shadow was no more.

Kael and Arwen stood in the clearing, their magic still swirling around them, their bodies exhausted but triumphant. The land was quiet, the sky now clear, the darkness replaced by a new dawn. The threat had passed, but the cost of the battle was evident in the exhaustion on their faces and the silence that hung between them.

"You were right," Kael said, his voice hoarse. "Strength alone couldn't defeat it."

Arwen nodded, her eyes filled with a wisdom born from centuries of living in harmony with the land. "We needed more than just our magic. We needed to let go of our hatred, our pride. Only by uniting could we banish the darkness."

Kael glanced at her, his gaze softening. "Perhaps there is more to this than I realized."

And so, in that quiet moment, amidst the ruins of the battle, the first true friendship between a unicorn and a dragon was forged. They had faced the darkness together, not as enemies, but as allies—each learning that the greatest strength lies not in the power of one, but in the unity of all.

The lesson was clear: even the greatest of enemies can become the most powerful of allies when they cast aside their differences and fight for something greater than themselves. And sometimes, the true power to defeat darkness lies not in strength, but in love and unity.

# Unicorn's Embrace

The winds were unusually still the night that young Sienna wandered deep into the woods. She had always been drawn to the forest at the edge of the village, where the trees were thick and ancient, and the whispers of the past seemed to float through the leaves like forgotten songs. But tonight felt different. It was the night of the full moon, and the air was heavy with an energy she couldn't explain.

She was an orphan, raised by the village's kind-hearted elders after her parents had died in a mysterious accident years ago. Though the village cared for her, Sienna often felt alone. She had never known the warmth of a family, only the distant affection of those who took pity on her and the empty spaces of her heart that seemed too wide to fill. The other children had their parents, their homes filled with laughter and love, while she had only memories of a past she could barely remember.

As Sienna wandered through the forest, her bare feet brushing the cool earth, she suddenly stopped. A soft glow appeared between the trees, brighter than the moonlight, pulsating like a heartbeat. Curiosity tugged at her, and despite her better judgment, she followed the light until she came to a small clearing.

In the center of the clearing stood a unicorn.

It was unlike anything Sienna had ever seen. Its coat was a shimmering silver, its mane flowing like liquid moonlight, and its horn—long and spiraled—glowed with a gentle radiance. The unicorn stood tall, its large, intelligent eyes fixed on her with an understanding that seemed to pierce her very soul.

For a moment, time seemed to stand still. The world around her faded into the background, and all that remained was the unicorn and its presence. She could feel the warmth of its magic, wrapping around her like a protective embrace.

"You've come," the unicorn spoke, its voice like a soft breeze, both melodic and knowing.

Sienna's heart skipped a beat. "You can talk?"

The unicorn nodded, its expression kind yet solemn. "I can. And I've been waiting for you. You see, Sienna, you've been chosen."

Sienna blinked in confusion. "Chosen? For what?"

The unicorn stepped forward, its hooves making no sound on the forest floor. "I have the power to grant you one wish. Anything you desire. A family, a home, a place where you belong."

Sienna's breath caught in her throat. A family? The thought of it seemed like a dream—one so far removed from her reality that it felt almost impossible. She had always wanted a family, someone to call her own, someone to love her without pity or obligation. But as the words hung in the air, she hesitated. There was something about the unicorn's gaze that made her question the weight of the wish.

"What's the catch?" she asked, her voice soft.

The unicorn tilted its head, a hint of sadness in its eyes. "There is no catch, child. But the wish will not give you what you think it will. You must choose wisely, for family is not simply a place or a name. It is a bond, a connection that can only be understood when you look beyond what you think you need."

Sienna felt a surge of emotion—hope, longing, confusion. She had dreamed of a family for as long as she could remember. A mother, a father, a place where she could feel whole. It was all she had ever wanted. She thought of the elders who had raised her, of the love they had shown her, but there was always something missing. She had never felt like she truly belonged, never felt the warmth of a true family.

"I want to belong," Sienna said, her voice breaking. "I want a family—people who love me, who will always be there."

The unicorn gazed at her for a long moment, as though considering her words. "You wish for love. For a home, a place where you are wanted. But be careful, child. Sometimes, the things we wish for are not the things we truly need."

Sienna nodded eagerly, not fully understanding but trusting in the unicorn's wisdom. She wanted a family, and that was all that mattered.

The unicorn stepped closer, its horn glowing brighter as it lowered its head toward her. A warm light enveloped her, and for a moment, Sienna felt the deepest peace she had ever known. It was as though every worry, every doubt, every feeling of loneliness was being washed away.

"You will have your wish," the unicorn said softly. "But remember, family is not always what it seems. It is not just a name, a place, or a thing—it is a choice, a commitment, and an understanding that goes beyond what the eyes can see."

The light faded, and Sienna opened her eyes, finding herself standing in a small, cozy house. The walls were warm with the glow of a fire, and a table was set for a meal. At the table sat a man and a woman, smiling at her with warmth and affection. They looked familiar—like figures from her past—but she couldn't place them.

"Come, sit," the woman said, her voice gentle. "Dinner is ready, my dear."

Sienna blinked, unsure of what was happening. She had wished for a family, but this felt... different. These people, though kind, felt distant, like strangers wearing the mask of familiarity. She sat at the table, her hands shaking slightly as they passed her a plate of food.

"This is your home now," the man said. "You're safe here. We'll take care of you."

But Sienna's heart was heavy. She didn't feel the connection she had imagined. These people were not her family—not truly. They had provided a place, a roof, but they hadn't filled the void inside her. She could see now that what she had longed for wasn't just a place to belong—it was a bond that came from love, from understanding, from shared experiences.

As the meal progressed, Sienna realized the truth. The unicorn had granted her a home, but it had not given her the family she truly needed. A family was not a place or a name. It was a relationship built on mutual love, trust, and understanding—not just the mere presence of people.

The next morning, Sienna returned to the forest, her heart full of both gratitude and sorrow. She found the unicorn once more, waiting for her by the edge of the meadow.

"I see now," she said softly, her voice steady. "It wasn't just about the family I wanted. It was about the love and connection I had to find, the people who would truly understand me."

The unicorn nodded, its eyes filled with compassion. "You've learned, child. Sometimes, the most important thing we can do is choose the family that chooses us—not just the one we wish for."

And as Sienna walked away from the clearing, she knew that the unicorn's embrace had given her more than just a wish—it had given her the understanding of what it truly meant to belong. It was a lesson she would carry with her, one that would guide her toward the family she was destined to find, not through magic, but through the love she gave and received.

# The Crystal Horn

The night sky over the Kingdom of Eldara was unlike any other. The stars, as ancient as the land itself, glittered like scattered jewels across a velvet cloth, while the moon cast its silver glow over the rolling hills. Beneath the moonlight, a lone figure walked quietly through the forest—a unicorn named Seraphiel. Her coat was as white as the snow on the highest mountain peaks, and her mane flowed like liquid light. But it was her horn that was the most extraordinary. Unlike any other unicorn, Seraphiel's horn was made entirely of crystal, its facets reflecting the moonlight in dazzling patterns.

Seraphiel had known for as long as she could remember that her horn was special, that it held the key to something ancient and powerful. She had never truly understood what that key unlocked, but the legends spoke of an ancient kingdom—one lost to time and hidden beneath the earth, its magic bound by a force greater than even the unicorns. Only the Crystal Horn could awaken it.

The forest was quiet as Seraphiel approached the sacred stone circle at the heart of the woods. The air here was thick with magic, old magic—magic that had waited for centuries. Her steps were silent as she moved toward the largest stone, a monolith that towered over the others, etched with runes that glowed faintly in the moonlight. This stone, known only to a few, was said to be the entrance to the Kingdom of Eldara, sealed long ago by the ancient rulers of the land.

Seraphiel reached up with her crystal horn and touched it to the stone. The moment the tip made contact, a surge of energy coursed through her body. The air around her shimmered, and the ground trembled beneath her hooves. The runes on the stone glowed brighter, their ancient meaning becoming clear. The stone was not simply a marker; it was a seal, a lock that could only be undone by the horn of crystal.

As the energy built, Seraphiel stepped back, her breath coming in shallow gasps. The ground before her cracked open, revealing a swirling vortex of light and shadow. The entrance to the hidden kingdom had been opened, but there was something in the air—an unease, a hesitation. Seraphiel had always known that the Kingdom of Eldara was not just a place of magic, but of great consequence. The kingdom had vanished for a reason, its rulers having made choices that had affected the very balance of the world. And now, for the first time in centuries, the door to that kingdom was open, and Seraphiel was about to enter.

But before she could take a step forward, a voice echoed from the darkness.

"You are brave to seek what was lost, unicorn," the voice said, smooth and cold. "But do you truly understand the cost of what you awaken?"

Seraphiel turned sharply, her ears twitching as she sought the source of the voice. From the shadows of the trees emerged a figure, cloaked in a flowing black robe. It was a man, though his face was hidden beneath the folds of his hood. He stood still, watching her with eyes that gleamed with a knowing light.

"What is this place?" Seraphiel asked, her voice steady but tinged with caution. "Why has it remained hidden for so long?"

The man stepped forward, his presence imposing. "This is the Kingdom of Eldara," he said, his voice low and resonant. "It was a kingdom of immense power, built upon the magic of the land, its people living in harmony with the world around them. But their ambition grew too great, their thirst for power too insatiable. The kingdom was destroyed, its rulers sealed away, and its magic locked by the very force that created it."

Seraphiel felt a shiver run down her spine. The stories had never been this vivid, never this real. She had always thought the kingdom's fall was a distant myth, a tale told to warn against the dangers of unchecked power. But now, standing at the edge of the kingdom's threshold, it felt much more real than she had imagined.

"You are not the first to seek the power of Eldara," the man continued, stepping closer. "But none have succeeded in wielding it without being consumed. The kingdom's power is a curse, not a gift. Those who seek to claim it must pay the price for the sins of the past."

Seraphiel lifted her head, her eyes flashing with determination. "I seek not power, but understanding. The world has changed. The balance is shifting, and I must know what lies in this kingdom before it's too late."

The man's eyes narrowed. "You believe you are different? That you can control what was once uncontrollable? You are but one creature in a world of chaos. The kingdom's magic cannot be controlled. It cannot be wielded."

Seraphiel stepped forward, her crystal horn glowing softly, its light reflecting the determination in her eyes. "I will see for myself."

With a powerful movement, Seraphiel entered the vortex. The world around her twisted and warped as the light swallowed her whole. When she emerged, she found herself standing in the heart of a grand hall. The walls were adorned with tapestries depicting scenes of celestial beings and kingdoms long forgotten, their faces blurred with time. The air was thick with an ancient, almost oppressive magic. The kingdom was not just a place—it was a living thing, pulsing with the echoes of a thousand years of history.

She looked around, taking in the towering pillars and the intricate carvings in the stone. At the far end of the hall stood a throne, its seat empty. She felt drawn to it, compelled to approach, and as she did, a soft whisper reached her ears.

"You are the heir of Eldara," the whisper said. "You are the one who will decide whether this kingdom will rise again, or whether it will remain buried forever."

Seraphiel's heart skipped a beat. She had not expected this. She had come seeking knowledge, not a legacy. She had always believed she was just a unicorn, one of many, with no more significance than the stars in the sky. But now, the weight of the kingdom's history, its burden, was upon her.

She turned to the man, who had followed her into the hall. He stood in the shadows, watching her with a knowing look. "The crystal horn is not just a key, unicorn," he said. "It is a symbol of what was lost. You are its true heir. The magic of Eldara belongs to you, but you must choose whether to embrace it or leave it sealed forever."

Seraphiel stood still, the weight of his words settling into her bones. She had come seeking knowledge, but what had she truly found? The kingdom's power was not meant for any one creature—it was a force beyond her control, one that had caused the destruction of a world long ago. But in that moment, she realized something: power, even the most powerful magic, was not about control. It was about responsibility, about understanding the consequences of what one sought.

She closed her eyes, the light of her crystal horn flickering softly. "The magic of Eldara must remain sealed," she said, her voice clear. "The past cannot be undone. The kingdom's power cannot be wielded again."

The man nodded, as though he had expected this answer. "You have learned the lesson of Eldara, unicorn. You have chosen wisely."

With that, the magic of the kingdom faded, the walls crumbling to dust, and the throne was no more. Seraphiel stood alone in the forest once more, the moonlight shining down upon her. The kingdom was gone, its power locked away, but the lesson remained within her heart: true strength lies not in the desire for power, but in the wisdom to know when to let it go.

# The Young Unicorn's Trial

The sun hung low over the forest, casting its golden light over the ancient grove where the unicorns gathered. The air was thick with the scent of moss and earth, and the trees stretched high, their boughs intertwined in a silent celebration of time's passing. Among the unicorns, there was a quiet sense of reverence, for today was no ordinary day. It was the day of the Trials, a rite of passage that every young unicorn had to face to prove themselves worthy of joining the council of the Elders, the wise and ancient unicorns who guided the land with their knowledge and magic.

Seraphina, a young unicorn whose coat shimmered like the dawn, stood at the edge of the clearing. Her heart pounded in her chest as she gazed at the circle of Elders gathered before her. They were the oldest of their kind, their horns glowing with centuries of magic and their eyes filled with knowledge that Seraphina could barely begin to understand. She had trained for this moment her entire life, but as the day of the Trials arrived, doubt gnawed at her.

"Seraphina, step forward," said Elder Alaris, the leader of the council. His voice was soft, like the rustle of leaves in a gentle breeze, but it carried the weight of authority. "The Trials are a measure of your strength, your wisdom, and your heart. Show us that you are ready to join us."

Seraphina took a deep breath and stepped forward, her hooves light against the soft earth. The Elders watched her closely, their eyes unreadable. She stood before them, her body tense, her mind racing with uncertainty. She had been told all her life that this moment would come, that she would have to prove her worth, but now that it was here, the pressure felt suffocating.

"The first trial is the Trial of Strength," Elder Alaris continued. "You must cross the River of Shadows, a place where the currents are fierce and the waters conceal many dangers. You will be tested on your resolve. Are you prepared?"

Seraphina nodded, though her legs trembled slightly beneath her. She had heard stories of the River of Shadows, a place where the magic of the land grew dark and twisted, where the waters could play tricks on even the strongest of minds. But she knew she had no choice. She had to pass this trial.

Without another word, Seraphina turned and walked toward the river's edge. The water before her was dark and swirling, its surface covered in mist that seemed to rise from the depths themselves. She could feel the weight of the magic within it, a pull that threatened to consume her.

With a deep breath, Seraphina stepped into the river. The cold water rushed against her legs, and the current tugged at her with surprising force. She focused, gathering her strength, but as she moved deeper, the water seemed to take on a life of its own. Shadows rose from the depths, whispering her name, calling to her, promising her things she had longed for—peace, acceptance, power. But Seraphina ignored them. She had been trained to resist these temptations, to focus on the task at hand.

The water roared as the shadows tried to pull her under, but Seraphina kept moving, one step at a time, her eyes fixed on the distant shore. She could feel the fear gnawing at her, but she pushed it aside, drawing on the strength that had always been within her. After what felt like an eternity, she reached the other side, her body drenched and exhausted, but she had passed the first trial.

The Elders watched her in silence, their expressions unreadable. Elder Alaris spoke again. "You have passed the Trial of Strength, but the second trial will test your mind. You must enter the Cave of Illusions, where the walls are lined with the memories of all who have entered before you. You will see things—things that may not be true. Your task is to distinguish the illusion from reality. Do you accept this challenge?"

Seraphina nodded again, though this trial seemed even more daunting. The Cave of Illusions was a place of confusion, where the mind was often tricked into seeing things that were not real. She had always been strong, but her mind? That was something different. She had struggled with doubts and insecurities for as long as she could remember.

With a single glance from Elder Alaris, she was led to the cave's entrance. The air inside was thick with the scent of stone and ancient magic, and as she stepped deeper into the darkness, the shadows closed in around her. The walls seemed to pulse, filled with whispers of forgotten memories, and strange shapes danced in the corners of her vision.

"Do not listen," a voice echoed in the darkness. "You are not strong enough. You will fail. You are nothing."

Seraphina stopped. The voice was her own, twisted and distorted, speaking the lies she had always feared to be true. For a moment, she hesitated, feeling the weight of her own insecurities rise up around her. The illusions were powerful, and it was so tempting to believe them. But then she remembered the river—the strength she had found in herself, the strength that had carried her through the darkness. She could not let these illusions control her.

Taking a deep breath, Seraphina focused on her inner light, the glow that had always been with her, the magic that came from within. She closed her eyes and ignored the whispers, focusing instead on the truth she knew in her heart: she was capable. She was worthy. And she was not alone.

The shadows receded, the illusions faded, and the cave grew still. She had passed the second trial.

When she emerged from the cave, the Elders were waiting. Elder Alaris nodded approvingly. "You have passed the Trial of the Mind, but the final trial is the Trial of the Heart. You must face the one thing that has always held you back—yourself. You must face the truth about who you are and what you truly seek."

Seraphina stood in silence. This was the hardest trial of all. She had spent her life struggling with the idea that she was not enough, that she would never be as wise or as strong as the Elders. Her heart had always carried the weight of self-doubt. But now, standing before them, she realized the truth: the only thing holding her back was her fear of not being enough. She had already proven her strength, her wisdom, her resolve. What she needed now was to embrace who she truly was.

With a deep breath, Seraphina stepped forward, her heart calm and steady. "I am enough. I am worthy," she whispered to herself, and as the words left her lips, the magic of the forest surged around her, wrapping her in a warm, golden light.

Elder Alaris stepped forward, his eyes filled with approval. "You have passed the final trial, Seraphina. You are ready to join the council of the Elders."

And as Seraphina looked around at the council of unicorns, she realized that the greatest lesson of all was not in proving her strength or wisdom. It was in embracing her own truth, and in knowing that to be part of something greater, she first had to accept herself.

# Unicorn in the Snow

The snow had been falling relentlessly for days, blanketing the small town of Ashford in a heavy, unyielding silence. The streets, usually bustling with life, now lay deserted, save for the occasional figure huddled under a thick coat, hurriedly moving from one building to the next. Winter had come early this year, and it seemed as though the season was determined to never leave.

Inside the town's modest homes, families sat close to flickering fires, the warmth of the flames a stark contrast to the cold that howled outside. For most, the winter had become an ordeal—something to endure until spring's distant promise. But for one resident, a young woman named Elara, it was an oppressive silence that wore at her soul.

Elara had lived in Ashford all her life, but the town no longer felt like home. The death of her parents two winters ago had left her isolated, with little family and even fewer friends. She worked long hours at the town's general store, keeping to herself, avoiding the discomfort of forced socializing, and the long stares from the townspeople who never quite knew how to approach someone who had lost so much.

That evening, as the town lay still beneath its blanket of snow, Elara took her usual solitary walk through the streets. She made her way toward the edge of town, to the woods that bordered Ashford. The trees stood bare, their limbs twisting like gnarled fingers reaching toward the dark sky. She often walked this path, where the wind whispered through the branches, carrying with it the scent of pine and earth. But tonight, the air was thick with something different, something that stirred a sense of hope she hadn't felt in years.

As she walked deeper into the woods, the snow around her began to glow faintly, a soft golden hue that flickered like candlelight. She stopped, her breath caught in her throat, and looked around. The world was bathed in a strange warmth, as though the winter itself had softened its grip. And then, through the trees, she saw it.

A figure, unlike anything she had ever seen, stood in the clearing ahead. It was a unicorn, its coat gleaming white, its mane flowing like silver threads under the moonlight. The creature's horn shimmered with an ethereal glow, casting ripples of light across the snow-covered ground.

Elara froze, her heart racing in disbelief. She had heard the old stories—the legends of unicorns, creatures of magic and purity—but they had always been nothing more than myths. Yet here, standing before her in the snowy clearing, was the very creature from those ancient tales.

The unicorn turned its head, locking eyes with her. There was something in its gaze—something deep and knowing—that seemed to reach beyond the surface, as though it could see into the very heart of her.

"Why are you here?" Elara whispered, her voice trembling. The wind had stopped, and for a moment, everything was still, as though the world was waiting for an answer.

The unicorn took a step forward, its hooves leaving soft imprints in the snow. And then, to Elara's astonishment, it spoke, its voice gentle but clear.

"I've come to bring you warmth," it said, "not just to your body, but to your heart."

Elara's breath caught in her chest. The words seemed impossible, but they filled her with a strange, comforting warmth. She stepped closer, drawn to the creature that seemed to radiate light, as though the very essence of magic lived within it.

"Why me?" she asked softly, unable to tear her eyes away from the unicorn's mesmerizing gaze. "What do I have to offer that you would come all this way for?"

The unicorn's eyes softened, as if it understood the weight of her question. "You have suffered, Elara. The cold you feel is not just from the winter's bite, but from the silence in your heart. I am here to remind you that warmth and light are not just found in the seasons, but in the love and connection we choose to share."

The unicorn's words struck her like a wave, pulling her back to memories of her parents—of laughter shared by the hearth, of the warmth of family gatherings. She had lost so much in the years since their death, and the winter had seemed to stretch on endlessly, echoing the emptiness inside her.

"You're not alone," the unicorn continued, as if sensing her thoughts. "Even in the coldest of winters, there is a spark of light, waiting to be rekindled."

Elara felt the sting of tears in her eyes, but she didn't look away from the unicorn. For the first time in a long time, she felt a flicker of something—hope, maybe, or something more elusive.

The unicorn stepped closer, nuzzling her gently with its horn, and a surge of warmth flooded her chest, as though the creature's very presence had reignited the light she had long buried. She felt a rush of emotions—grief, longing, and a quiet peace she hadn't known in years.

"Your heart has been frozen, Elara," the unicorn said, "but it need not stay that way. The warmth you seek is within you, within the love you still carry for those you've lost, and for the life that remains."

As the unicorn's words settled into her heart, Elara realized something. It wasn't that the winter had come to stay—it was that she had let it linger too long, holding on to the grief and the cold that had filled her life. The warmth, the love, was still there, waiting for her to embrace it once more.

"Thank you," Elara whispered, the words barely escaping her lips. She reached out, and to her surprise, the unicorn nuzzled her again, a deep, comforting warmth filling her chest.

When she finally looked up, the unicorn was fading, its form dissolving into the snow as if it had never been there. But the warmth remained, a soft glow that lingered in her heart. As she walked back toward the village, the world felt different. The snow no longer felt cold and isolating—it was beautiful, soft, and quiet, like a blanket that wrapped her in its embrace.

The next morning, when Elara woke to find the snow still falling gently outside her window, the world seemed a little brighter, the air a little warmer. She knew that the unicorn's visit was a gift, a reminder that even in the harshest winters, warmth could be found—not just in the magic of the world around her, but in the love she chose to give and receive.

And as she walked through the streets of Ashford, greeting the villagers she had once avoided, she realized that the warmth she had been seeking had never been far away. It had always been within her reach—waiting to melt the ice of isolation, to rekindle the light of connection. She smiled softly, knowing that the magic she had found in the snow was not just the gift of a unicorn, but the gift she could give herself.

# The Unicorn's Moonlight Ride

Every full moon, the town of Evershade would fall into an expectant silence. The villagers, with their eyes lifted toward the heavens, would wait, knowing that tonight was the night—the night the unicorn would run. It had been this way for as long as the oldest among them could remember. The legend spoke of a unicorn whose silver coat shone like moonlight itself, galloping across the sky, bringing peace and magic to the world below. But it wasn't just the beauty of the unicorn's flight that enchanted the people of Evershade. It was the sense of wonder it inspired, the reminder that the impossible could exist.

And so, when the moon rose high in the sky on the first full moon of spring, the villagers gathered as they always did, their eyes tracking the sky in reverence. They had seen the unicorn many times, but every time, the sight was as breathtaking as the last.

This time, however, something was different.

The unicorn appeared as always, its gleaming form silhouetted against the silver glow of the full moon. Its mane shimmered like liquid stardust, and its horn spiraled with radiant light. As it galloped through the sky, the town below seemed to brighten, bathed in an otherworldly glow. The wind carried the echo of hooves, soft and musical, as though the unicorn were singing in its own language.

But tonight, something strange happened. As the unicorn reached the highest point in its flight, a ripple ran through the air. It was barely noticeable at first, a faint distortion, as if the very fabric of the sky had been disturbed. The unicorn faltered mid-gallop, its hooves hesitating in the air. Then, with a sudden force, a shadow stretched across the moon, eclipsing its light for the briefest of moments.

The villagers below gasped in confusion and fear, watching as the unicorn veered to the side, its graceful flight thrown off course. It pawed at the air, a small whinny of distress escaping its lips as it began to spiral downward, struggling to regain control.

From the heart of the darkness that had blocked the moon, a figure emerged—flickering, like a shadow caught in a gust of wind. It was tall, its form undefined, wrapped in an aura of strange, shifting energy that twisted and pulsed like a storm. The unicorn fought to ascend, its wings beating hard, but the shadow seemed to pull at it, tugging it downward.

A strange coldness settled over the town. The villagers looked up, paralyzed with fear as the shadow crept closer, its tendrils stretching out like fingers reaching for the heart of the unicorn. They had heard the whispers, the old stories about the things that existed beyond the veil, things that would come for the light whenever it shined too brightly. They had never thought it was true—until now.

The unicorn's light flickered, its power waning under the pressure of the dark force that sought to envelop it. And then, as suddenly as it had appeared, the shadow's form twisted and writhed, an unnatural force that seemed to feed on the very light the unicorn radiated. With one final cry, the unicorn fought against the pull of the darkness. It plunged toward the earth below, its light diminishing, leaving behind only a faint, shimmering trail.

In the village, the air thickened. A profound silence followed. The people stared in horror, unsure of what had just occurred. They had witnessed the unicorn's flight many times before, but never like this. Something was wrong. Something had changed.

And then, out of the silence, a voice broke through—a voice soft, almost imperceptible, like the sound of wind passing through ancient trees.

"Do not fear," the voice said.

The villagers turned, searching for the source. It was an old woman, standing at the edge of the clearing, her hands clasped together. Her silver hair glimmered in the dim moonlight, and her eyes—deep and wise—seemed to see beyond the world itself.

"The unicorn has not fallen," she said, her voice carrying with an unexpected strength. "It has only been tested. This is the trial of the moon's passage. The light must sometimes be hidden, so that it may emerge again, brighter than before."

The villagers exchanged confused glances. What did she mean? The unicorn had always flown free, always shining, never faltering.

The old woman stepped forward, her gaze never leaving the sky. "What you saw tonight was not a failure," she continued. "It was a reminder. The light—true light—does not shine without darkness. The unicorn runs not just to bring light, but to navigate the shadows that lie between."

As she spoke, the sky began to clear. The moonlight broke through the clouds again, casting a pale glow over the village. Slowly, steadily, the unicorn's light returned, stronger than before. It emerged from the shadows, not from the depths of the night, but from the very heart of it. Its silver mane sparkled as it once had, more brilliant now, with a power that seemed to hum through the air.

The unicorn broke free of the shadow's hold and soared higher, its light blinding in its radiance. It moved across the sky with renewed strength, its power undeniable, a symbol of resilience and balance.

The villagers watched in awe as the unicorn ascended, its form now a beacon of hope against the vast expanse of darkness. The shadows had not defeated it; they had merely tested its strength, reminding it of the balance between light and dark.

The old woman turned to the crowd, her smile serene. "Do not be afraid of the darkness," she said. "For it is the shadow that allows the light to shine brighter. Without it, the light would be but a flicker. It is only in embracing the dark that we can truly understand the power of the light."

As the unicorn's final gallop faded into the horizon, the villagers stood in silence, a sense of peace settling over them. The moonlight was as it should be, full and pure. And for the first time in a long while, the villagers understood something they had always taken for granted: the light would always return, but only after it had fought its way through the darkness.

The lesson was clear—sometimes, to move forward, to grow stronger, we must first confront the shadows. And only then, with the strength gained from the struggle, can we truly shine.

# The Unicorn's Last Dance

In a time long forgotten by most, unicorns had roamed the earth freely, their shimmering coats reflecting the light of the stars, their horns imbued with ancient magic. They were creatures of grace and wonder, protectors of nature, embodiments of purity and beauty. But the world had changed. The forests had been chopped down, the mountains mined for riches, and the once-vibrant meadows had been replaced by cities of steel and glass. And with the changing world came the fading of magic. One by one, the unicorns had disappeared, their presence slipping away like a dream upon waking.

But there was one unicorn left.

Her name was Lysandra, and she had lived longer than most could comprehend. She had witnessed the rise and fall of kingdoms, the birth of empires, and the loss of magic that had once flowed freely through the world. She was the last of her kind, the final spark of an ancient flame that had nearly extinguished. Now, in a world that no longer believed in the impossible, Lysandra wandered alone.

She had seen the signs of her kind's extinction—humans no longer saw magic in the world; they no longer looked to the stars and the moon with wonder. In their pursuit of progress, they had lost touch with the natural world, and in doing so, they had lost the ability to believe in the extraordinary. The forests that had once thrived with life were now mere echoes of their former selves. And so, Lysandra had decided that it was time to say goodbye. One last dance, under the stars, would be her final gift to the world she had once shared with so many others.

The moon rose high above the horizon, casting its pale light across the empty fields where Lysandra had spent countless nights dancing. The world around her was quiet, the usual sounds of life replaced by the stillness that only came when magic was fading. She stood in the center of the meadow, the soft breeze ruffling her mane, and closed her eyes.

She could feel the energy of the earth beneath her hooves, the rhythm of the world still pulsing faintly. For a moment, she allowed herself to remember—the joy of galloping through the forests, the laughter of the other unicorns, the vibrant energy that had once flowed through her every movement.

With a deep breath, she lifted her head and looked to the heavens. The stars sparkled above her like distant memories, a reminder of all the magic that had been lost. And then, with a single graceful movement, she began to dance.

It was slow at first, tentative, as if testing the waters of a world that no longer seemed to hold magic. But as she moved, the energy of the earth began to respond to her—soft at first, but with growing intensity. The ground beneath her hooves began to glow faintly, a soft light rising from the earth itself, following her as she twirled in the moonlight. Lysandra's movements became more fluid, more certain, as though the magic of the world, hidden for so long, was slowly awakening in response to her dance. Her hooves tapped lightly against the earth, sending ripples of light through the grass, and her mane flowed like silver, catching the light of the stars.

For hours, Lysandra danced beneath the sky, lost in the rhythm of the world, moving in time with the pulsing energy that she had always known but had almost forgotten. She danced as if no one were watching, as if there were still a world full of creatures to share her magic with, to celebrate life with. Her horn glowed softly, a beacon of light in the darkness, casting its glow across the meadow and into the sky. She was the last of her kind, and yet, in that moment, she felt as though she were part of something greater than herself—a last echo of a world that had once been.

But as the night wore on, the dance began to slow. Lysandra could feel the energy within her fading, the light of her horn dimming. The magic of the earth, though powerful, was not enough to sustain her forever. She had given everything she had—her energy, her spirit, her magic—and now it was time to rest.

As she slowed, the meadow fell silent again. The light of her horn flickered and faded, and the glowing earth around her dimmed. Lysandra collapsed to her knees, the weight of the world pressing down on her. She closed her eyes for a moment, her head resting against the soft grass. In that moment, she felt at peace. She had given everything she could. Her dance had been a tribute to the magic that still lingered in the world, a final act of defiance against the fading of the light. She had brought a spark of wonder back into a world that had forgotten what it meant to dream.

And then, something unexpected happened.

A soft sound broke the silence, a sound that felt like the heartbeat of the earth itself. The ground beneath her stirred, the air around her began to shimmer once more, and for a moment, Lysandra's heart skipped. She lifted her head, her tired eyes searching the meadow. The light that had dimmed began to brighten again, the magic returning in waves, as if the world itself were responding to her final act of grace.

Slowly, from the shadows at the edge of the meadow, a figure emerged. It was not a unicorn—no, it was something different. It was a child, no older than eight or nine, with eyes full of wonder and a smile that spoke of a world still full of magic. In their hand, they held a small crystal, glowing faintly with a light that seemed to match Lysandra's own.

The child walked toward her, eyes wide with awe, and placed the crystal gently on the ground at Lysandra's feet. The unicorn's breath caught in her chest. The child's presence, though unexpected, felt familiar—like a long-lost memory awakening.

With the child's touch, the crystal pulsed, and the energy around them surged once more. The child stepped back, and the meadow, the earth, the very air seemed to come alive, the magic swirling around them both. Lysandra stood slowly, her strength returning as the earth itself seemed to fill her again with light. The dance was not over. The magic had not been lost—it had only been waiting.

The lesson was clear: magic never truly fades, not entirely. It lives in the hearts of those who still believe, in the hands of those who remember the wonder of the world. Lysandra had danced, not to celebrate an end, but to ignite a spark that would carry her kind's magic into the future, where it would be reborn.

And as she looked into the child's eyes, Lysandra knew that though she was the last of her kind, she was not the end. The magic would continue, as long as someone believed in the dance.

# The Unicorn and the Lost Star

The night the star fell, the entire valley seemed to hold its breath. It had been a night like any other—quiet, serene, with the silver glow of the moon bathing the world in its soft light. But then, with a crackling burst of energy that sent a ripple through the air, the star descended, plunging from the heavens and landing on the soft grass near the edge of the forest. The light from the fallen star was blinding for a moment, but as the glow faded, a small, fragile shape could be seen nestled within the grass: the star, now a shimmering crystal, lay in the earth, glowing faintly, its warmth radiating outward.

For days, no one dared approach it. The villagers spoke of it in hushed tones, fearful of the unknown magic it might carry. It wasn't the first time a star had fallen, but it was the first time one had landed so close. Among the creatures of the valley, there was one who had always held a special connection to the stars—a unicorn named Elara. Her coat shimmered like the night sky itself, and her horn sparkled with the light of a thousand forgotten dreams. Elara had always been drawn to the stars, feeling their distant pull as if they were part of her own spirit. And when she heard of the fallen star, she knew her destiny was tied to it.

On the evening of the third day, Elara ventured into the valley where the star lay, her hooves light upon the earth. As she approached the glowing crystal, she could feel its warmth radiating against her skin. The star pulsed gently, its glow soft but steady. Kneeling beside it, Elara touched her horn to the crystal, her magic flowing through it, and as she did, she heard a voice—soft, distant, like the murmur of a dream.

"Return me," it whispered, "return me to the sky."

The voice came not from the star itself, but from deep within her heart, as though it had always been there, waiting for her to hear. Elara knew then what she had to do. The star had fallen for a reason, and it was her task to see it returned to its rightful place in the heavens. But the journey would not be easy. The valley was full of dangers—wild forests, raging rivers, and mystical beings who guarded the lands beyond. She would need help.

With the crystal nestled gently against her side, Elara set off toward the mountains where the stars touched the earth. She traveled through dense forests and over rushing streams, her steps steady but thoughtful, knowing that every moment of her journey would bring her closer to the heart of the mystery. It wasn't long before she came across her first challenge.

At the edge of the forest stood an ancient oak, its branches twisted into grotesque shapes. The air around it shimmered with an unnatural stillness. From the shadow beneath the tree, a figure emerged—a dark creature with glowing eyes and a twisted grin. It was a shadow, more of a presence than a being, its form barely discernible against the night.

"Where do you think you're going, unicorn?" it asked, its voice a rasping whisper that seemed to echo in her mind.

Elara stood tall, her horn glowing softly. "I must return the star to the sky," she replied. "I must complete my journey."

The shadow laughed, a sound like dry leaves in the wind. "The sky? You think you can return what has fallen? What belongs to the heavens cannot be taken back so easily. The journey you seek is perilous, and you are not the first to attempt it."

Elara's gaze never wavered. "I do not fear the peril," she said. "But I will not let the star remain here. Its place is above, and I will see it returned."

The shadow stepped closer, its eyes gleaming with malice. "Then you must first defeat me," it hissed.

Without warning, the shadow lunged, its form twisting into a mass of darkness that swirled toward Elara. The unicorn's horn flared brightly as she called upon her magic, sending a pulse of light toward the shadow. The darkness recoiled, but it was not defeated. The battle between light and shadow raged on, Elara's strength ebbing with every strike. But she could feel the star growing warmer against her side, its energy feeding her resolve. With a final burst of light, the shadow disintegrated into nothing, its presence banished from the forest.

Exhausted but undeterred, Elara continued on, the star's pulse guiding her every step. As she neared the mountains, the air grew colder, the winds harsher. The path became treacherous, but she pressed forward, knowing that the sky was waiting for her.

At the summit of the highest mountain, Elara finally reached the place where the stars touched the earth. The sky above her was a canvas of endless black, dotted with countless stars. But there was something different tonight—something she hadn't expected. In the center of the sky, where the stars shone brightest, a dark void had formed, as if the heavens themselves were holding their breath.

Elara gazed upward, her heart heavy with the weight of her task. She approached the edge of the mountain, holding the star in her magic, and as she did, the void above her seemed to pulse, drawing closer. With one final, steadying breath, Elara raised the star high, her horn glowing with every ounce of power she could muster.

The star trembled, then slowly, it began to rise, its glow piercing through the darkness. As it ascended toward the heavens, the sky seemed to open, a path of light unfurling to welcome it. Elara watched as the star found its place among the others, the void in the sky closing as the star became one with the constellation it was meant to join.

But as the light of the star filled the sky, Elara felt a deep peace wash over her. It was not just the return of the star that mattered—it was the realization that the journey had changed her. She had traveled alone, facing countless dangers, yet she had never truly been alone. The magic of the star, the pull of the sky, had always been with her, guiding her, just as it had always been with the world. The star's journey was hers as well, and in returning it to the sky, she had found something greater than herself—something timeless, something that connected all things, whether seen or unseen.

And with the star safely in its place, Elara stood on the mountaintop, watching as the light of the sky filled the world around her. The journey had ended, but the magic of the universe, of the stars and the earth, would continue forever, reminding her that even in the darkest of nights, there was always a light waiting to be restored.

# The Forbidden Forest

In the heart of the valley, nestled between the steep mountains that reached toward the heavens, there was a forest that no creature dared enter. Known as the Forbidden Forest, it was whispered about in hushed tones, a place of danger and mystery. The trees grew thick and twisted, their gnarled roots entangling the earth in a web of darkness. The air there was thick with ancient magic, and it was said that anyone who ventured too deep would never return.

But for young Zephyr, none of that mattered. His best friend, a young doe named Liora, had fallen ill, struck by a mysterious affliction that no healer could cure. The village's only hope lay in a rare flower known to grow deep within the heart of the Forbidden Forest—the Silvermoon Blossom. It was a flower so rare and powerful that it could heal even the most grievous of wounds, lifting the most stubborn of curses. Zephyr had heard stories of its beauty and power for as long as he could remember, but he never thought he would need to find it—until now.

Liora's condition had worsened over the past few days. Her golden coat had dulled, and her once-bright eyes had become clouded with pain. The village healer had tried every known remedy, but nothing worked. Desperation had driven Zephyr to make a decision he never thought he would: he would enter the Forbidden Forest, face whatever dangers awaited, and retrieve the Silvermoon Blossom.

The sun was just beginning to set as Zephyr stepped into the forest's edge. The first thing he noticed was the silence. Even the birds had stopped singing, the wind no longer whispered through the trees. The only sound was his hooves, echoing off the moss-covered ground. He took a deep breath and pressed forward, ignoring the creeping fear in the pit of his stomach.

As he ventured deeper, the trees began to grow taller, their branches thick and intertwined, blocking out the fading light. The air grew heavy, thick with the scent of earth and decay. Every step felt like a journey into another world, where the laws of nature didn't seem to apply. He passed strange, glowing mushrooms and twisted vines that seemed to move of their own accord, their thorns gleaming like sharp daggers. His heart pounded in his chest, but Zephyr's resolve was unwavering. Liora's life was in his hooves, and he would not let fear stop him.

The deeper he went, the more the forest seemed to twist and bend around him. The path grew more treacherous, with thick roots rising from the ground like serpents, waiting to trip him. Strange shadows danced on the periphery of his vision, and eerie sounds echoed through the trees—soft whispers, like voices in a forgotten language. Zephyr kept his head low, his horn glowing faintly with the soft light of his magic, guiding him through the darkness.

As the night wore on, he began to feel a strange sense of being watched. He couldn't shake the feeling that the forest was alive, watching him, judging him. He pressed forward, determined not to turn back now. After what felt like hours, he reached a clearing. In the center of the clearing, bathed in a soft, otherworldly glow, stood a single plant. Its petals were silver, like moonlight itself, glimmering in the darkness. The Silvermoon Blossom.

Zephyr's heart soared at the sight. He had found it. The flower was even more beautiful than he had imagined, its petals delicate and shimmering in the moonlight. He stepped forward, his hooves brushing the ground gently, as if afraid to disturb the perfection before him. But as his horn neared the flower, a voice stopped him cold.

"Do you know what you seek, young one?" The voice was soft, feminine, yet powerful, resonating through the clearing like an ancient song.

Zephyr froze, his eyes searching the darkness. From the shadows stepped a figure—a woman, tall and ethereal, her skin pale as the moon and her hair like woven silver. She was clothed in flowing robes that shimmered like the stars, and her eyes, though soft, held an ancient wisdom.

"I seek the Silvermoon Blossom," Zephyr said, his voice steady despite the uncertainty in his heart. "My companion is ill, and this flower is the only thing that can save her."

The woman studied him for a moment, her gaze piercing yet calm. "The Silvermoon Blossom is a flower of great power," she said, her voice echoing in the stillness. "But it does not come without a price. It is a gift from the earth, meant to heal, but it also binds the one who takes it. To use its power is to forever change the one who carries it."

Zephyr's heart skipped. "I don't care what the cost is. I just want to save Liora."

The woman's expression softened. "You do not understand. Every choice you make here will have consequences. You may save your friend, but you will lose something precious in return."

Zephyr's gaze hardened with determination. "I am willing to pay any price to save her."

The woman studied him for a long moment, as if weighing the truth in his words. Finally, she nodded and stepped aside. "Then take the flower, but know that what you gain comes with a heavy cost."

Without hesitation, Zephyr reached out with his magic and gently plucked the Silvermoon Blossom from its stem. The moment his hooves touched the petals, a surge of energy rushed through him, overwhelming his senses. It was pure, radiant, a force unlike anything he had ever known. But as it coursed through him, something shifted. The glow of his horn dimmed, and he felt the weight of something being pulled from him.

As he turned to leave, the woman spoke again. "Remember, the price is never truly understood until it is paid."

Zephyr didn't look back. He raced through the forest, his mind focused only on Liora, on getting the flower back to her before it was too late. When he reached the village, he found her lying in the meadow, her body weak but breathing. He placed the Silvermoon Blossom at her side, and within moments, its magic took hold. Liora's golden coat returned to its vibrant hue, and her eyes fluttered open, clear and bright once again.

But Zephyr's joy was short-lived. As the magic of the flower faded, he realized something: the magic had taken more than it had given. His own coat, once shimmering and radiant, had dulled. His horn, once bright with light, was now pale and dull. He had saved Liora, but in doing so, he had given up his own magic. The price he had paid for the Silvermoon Blossom was not one of material cost, but of his very essence.

Liora looked up at him, her eyes filled with gratitude, but also confusion. "Zephyr... you're..."

"I'm fine," he said, his voice hollow. He forced a smile, but inside, he felt a deep emptiness. He had saved his friend, but in the process, he had lost something vital. The woman's words echoed in his mind: *Every choice you make here will have consequences.*

And as he looked at Liora, healed and whole, he realized that sometimes, the true cost of love is not the sacrifice of things, but of oneself.

# Unicorn's Promise

In the small village of Belmere, nestled between rolling hills and dense forests, there was a legend told by the fireside, passed from one generation to the next. It spoke of a unicorn, radiant and strong, who had once made a promise to a child—a promise to protect her, no matter the cost.

That child was Meira.

When Meira was just five years old, she had wandered deep into the woods beyond the village, drawn by the scent of wildflowers and the distant song of birds. Her parents, distracted by the evening chores, had not noticed her absence until it was too late. By then, the forest had swallowed her whole, and darkness had begun to creep in. Meira, with her small legs and curious heart, had no concept of the dangers lurking in the trees.

It was then, at the edge of the forest, when the shadows were beginning to stretch long, that the unicorn appeared.

He emerged from the mist like a creature from a dream, his coat as white as moonlight, his horn gleaming with a soft glow that made the night seem a little less dark. He was magnificent, his eyes full of ancient wisdom and kindness. Meira, frightened at first, instinctively reached out toward him, and without hesitation, the unicorn knelt before her. His voice, like the rustle of leaves, filled the air.

"I will protect you, little one," he said. "Always."

And so, for the years that followed, the unicorn kept his promise. Whenever Meira was in danger, whether from a harsh winter storm, a wild animal, or the dangers that sometimes lurked in the dark corners of the world, the unicorn was there. His presence was a constant comfort to her, a soft glow in the world of uncertainty.

As the years passed, the promise remained unbroken, and Meira grew up in the shadow of that protection. She blossomed into a young woman, her hair the color of autumn leaves, her eyes the color of the sky after a rainstorm. But with each passing year, something else changed. As the world became bigger, more complex, and more challenging, the safety of the forest and the steady presence of the unicorn began to feel more distant.

Meira began to understand the weight of the world, its harshness, its indifference. She had learned of love, loss, and heartache. She had fallen in love with a young man from the village, and with him, she had dreamed of leaving Belmere, seeking her own path. But always, in the back of her mind, was the unicorn—the creature who had protected her since childhood, who had always been there when she called.

One evening, as the sun dipped below the horizon, Meira stood at the edge of the forest, where it all began. She knew the unicorn was near, even though she couldn't see him. His presence was a whisper in the wind, the rustle of the trees.

"Why do you still follow me?" she asked aloud, her voice carrying into the twilight. "Why do you still protect me?"

A soft whinny echoed in response, and the unicorn stepped from the shadows, his silvery form almost glowing in the fading light.

"I made a promise, Meira," he said, his voice steady and strong, but with an edge of weariness. "A promise to you, to your heart. I will always protect you."

Meira looked at him, her brow furrowed with concern. "But I'm no longer a child. I've learned to take care of myself. I've lived through pain and loss, and I've survived. I don't need you the way I used to."

The unicorn's gaze softened, but there was a sadness in his eyes. "You've grown, yes. But that does not mean you do not need protection. The world can be cruel, and there are forces beyond your understanding that seek to bring harm."

Meira shook her head. "But it's not just the world I'm worried about. It's you. You've kept your promise for so long, but I can see it in your eyes—you're tired. You've watched me grow, and you've stayed beside me, even when I've strayed from the path you wanted for me."

The unicorn lowered his head, the weight of years pressing upon him. "I've been here, always. But I cannot protect you forever. My strength, my magic, is not infinite. There comes a time when even the brightest light must fade."

Meira felt a pang in her chest, realizing what he was truly saying. "Are you saying that you can't protect me anymore?"

The unicorn took a step forward, his horn brushing against her shoulder gently. "No. I'm not saying that. But you must understand, child, the promise I made was not just to keep you safe—it was to help you find your own strength. To protect you until you no longer needed me."

Tears welled in Meira's eyes, the weight of the moment heavy on her heart. "I need you, though. I always will."

The unicorn looked at her, his eyes full of compassion. "You always will, but not in the way you think. Protection is not just about shielding you from harm. It's about teaching you how to face the world on your own terms, with strength and grace. My promise was not to keep you sheltered—it was to help you find your wings."

Meira stepped back, her mind reeling. The unicorn's words echoed in her ears, but they were not what she had wanted to hear. She wanted him to remain by her side, as he always had. She wanted the certainty that he would always be there, an unshakable presence in her life.

But as she stood there, staring into his deep, knowing eyes, she realized that he was right. She had outgrown the need for constant protection. She had learned the lessons he had imparted to her all along—how to be strong, how to face adversity, how to carry the weight of the world with grace.

"I understand," she whispered, her voice trembling. "I understand now."

The unicorn's form shimmered faintly, and with a soft, final whinny, he began to fade, his presence retreating into the forest, back to where he had come from. But even as he disappeared from sight, Meira felt his warmth within her, like a flame that would never go out.

And as the moon rose high above the forest, Meira stood there alone, but not really alone. She had grown. And though the unicorn's promise had changed, it had not been broken. For the greatest gift he had given her was not just protection—it was the strength to face the world on her own.

# The Unicorn and the Garden of Wishes

In the heart of an ancient forest, hidden from the prying eyes of men, there was a garden unlike any other. It was known as the Garden of Wishes, a magical place where the very earth seemed to hum with possibility. The flowers here bloomed with colors that did not exist anywhere else, and the air was thick with the scent of dreams. Every leaf, every petal, held the promise of something extraordinary. To enter the garden was to step into a world where wishes came to life, where hopes were nurtured and desires granted.

And yet, for all its beauty, the garden was not a place meant for all. There were those who sought it for reasons less noble than the wish they longed for. Greed, jealousy, and desire for power often darkened the hearts of those who ventured too close. And so, the garden had its guardian—a unicorn named Arion.

Arion had been chosen for his strength, his purity, and his unwavering commitment to protecting the sacred space. His coat gleamed like the first light of dawn, and his horn shimmered with the magic of the garden itself. He had watched over the garden for centuries, ensuring that only those with pure hearts could approach, that only the deserving could have their wishes granted. But as time passed, Arion had begun to feel the weight of his duty. The garden had grown quieter, the air heavier. He could sense that something was wrong.

One evening, as the sun dipped below the horizon and the garden's magic began to pulse with the light of a thousand unseen stars, Arion heard the whisper of a presence. It was faint at first, like the rustling of leaves in a distant wind. But then it grew louder, darker. A figure moved at the edge of the garden, its shape obscured by shadows. Arion's horn flared to life, its light piercing the growing darkness.

"Who dares enter?" Arion called out, his voice steady, yet filled with an authority that seemed to echo through the trees. "This garden is not for those with selfish hearts."

From the shadows, a figure emerged—a man, cloaked in black, his face hidden beneath a hood. He moved with an unsettling grace, as though the darkness itself had wrapped around him. His eyes, when they met Arion's, glowed with an unnatural light, one that did not reflect the purity of the garden.

"I am here for what belongs to me," the figure said, his voice like a slow, creeping fog. "The wishes that you protect are mine to claim."

Arion's heart tightened. He had seen such figures before—those whose desire for power and control led them to seek out the garden's magic. But something about this one felt different. He radiated a darkness, a force that seemed to twist the very air around him.

"You have no right," Arion said, stepping forward. "This is a sacred place. It is not meant to be exploited by those who seek to bend its power to their will."

The figure smiled, though it was not a smile of joy. "Then I will take what I desire, whether you wish it or not."

With a wave of his hand, the air around him shimmered. The ground trembled, and the trees of the garden swayed as if caught in an unseen storm. Arion's heart raced. This was no ordinary intruder—this was a force of corruption, someone who sought to twist the wishes of the garden for their own gain. The unicorn's horn flared, its light shining brighter than the stars themselves, and the garden responded. Vines twisted upward from the earth, flowers bloomed with colors that pulsed like fire, and a protective barrier began to form around the heart of the garden.

But the figure was not deterred. He raised his hand again, and the darkness swirled around him, forming into tendrils that reached for the heart of the garden, seeking to choke its magic. Arion charged, his hooves pounding against the earth, his horn aimed at the dark figure.

The two forces collided with a crash that shook the ground beneath them. Light and shadow tangled in the air, each seeking to overpower the other.

For what felt like an eternity, the struggle raged on. Arion's magic fought against the darkness, pushing it back, but the figure seemed to draw strength from the very shadows he controlled. Arion could feel himself weakening, his energy drained with every wave of darkness that pressed against him. He had always been strong, but this power, this force, was something he had never faced before.

Finally, with one last surge of magic, Arion struck. His horn pierced through the tendrils of shadow, shattering the darkness with a burst of light. The figure let out a roar of frustration, falling back into the shadows from which he had come. The garden, once again, was bathed in light. The flowers bloomed with renewed brilliance, and the air hummed with the peaceful magic that had always defined the place.

But Arion, exhausted and wounded, sank to his knees. The fight had taken its toll. The garden had been saved, but at what cost? He could feel the magic of the place begin to fade, like the last breath of a dying star.

As he struggled to rise, a voice whispered in his mind. It was the voice of the garden, the voice of the wishes it held.

"You have done what was needed," the voice said, gentle and full of understanding. "But now, you must let go."

Arion's heart faltered. "Let go?" he whispered. "But I have protected this place for so long. I cannot leave it unguarded."

The voice was soft, but it carried a profound weight. "The garden no longer needs a guardian who holds it in the past. It needs a new keeper, one who can let the wishes flow freely, without the weight of old promises. You have protected it with love, but now you must trust that the garden will continue, in ways that are beyond your understanding."

Arion closed his eyes, his head bowed. He had always believed that the garden was his responsibility to protect, that it was his promise to keep. But now, he realized that his duty had always been to nurture the magic, to let it grow, to trust it to find its own path.

When he opened his eyes again, the dark figure was gone, and the garden had returned to its peaceful state. The wishes were safe, not because of his struggle, but because of the trust he had placed in the world. The garden, like the wishes it held, needed no single protector—it was part of the world, a piece of the great, ever-changing cycle.

And as Arion rose to his hooves, he realized the greatest lesson the garden had taught him: sometimes, the most powerful thing we can do is let go, to trust the world to unfold in its own way, knowing that the magic will always be there, waiting to bloom again.

# The Unicorn's Melody

The mountains of Eldras were known for their beauty, but also for their mystery. Jagged peaks reached into the sky, their snow-capped tips piercing the heavens like the fingers of some forgotten god. Valleys nestled between the ranges, their deep shadows holding secrets that only the wind seemed to know. It was a place where time moved differently, where old stories took root, and travelers seldom returned unchanged.

Ivor, a man weary from the hustle of the world, had come to the mountains seeking peace. A wanderer by nature, he had spent years chasing the next thrill, the next challenge, never stopping long enough to listen to the quiet whispers of his own soul. But something had drawn him to these mountains, an inexplicable pull, a calling that had haunted his nights for weeks before he packed his belongings and set off.

The journey had been long, and the climb up the mountainside was arduous. His feet ached, his body cried for rest, but the promise of something beyond the reach of ordinary men kept him moving. That was when he first heard it.

It was faint at first, like the rustling of leaves on the wind, a soft, haunting sound that seemed to drift on the air. He stopped in his tracks, tilting his head as the melody wound its way through the mountain pass. The sound was strange, beautiful in a way he couldn't describe. It had a resonance to it, as if it was both distant and yet as close as his own heartbeat. A song, or perhaps a call, a sound that seemed to beckon him forward.

He tried to dismiss it as a trick of the wind, but it grew louder, clearer. It was the unmistakable sound of a melody, ethereal and delicate, but full of depth. It tugged at something deep within him, something he had forgotten was there—a longing, a need to understand, to discover.

Driven by an urge he could not explain, Ivor pushed forward. The path grew steeper, and the melody grew clearer still. It was as though the mountains themselves were guiding him, urging him toward the source of the sound. His breath quickened, his heart beat faster, and with each step, the song seemed to wrap around him, drawing him deeper into its embrace.

By the time he reached the edge of a deep, mist-filled valley, he could hear the melody clearly, as though it were right beside him. His feet moved faster, his curiosity now an obsession. And then, through the fog, he saw it—a figure standing at the center of a clearing.

It was a unicorn.

Its coat was pure white, almost glowing against the shadows of the forest, and its horn, long and spiraled, shimmered with an iridescent light. The creature's eyes, deep and knowing, stared directly at Ivor as though it had been expecting him. But it was the sound that captivated him. The unicorn was not merely standing there—it was singing, its voice carrying the haunting melody that had led him here.

The air around them seemed to vibrate with magic, the trees swaying as though the very earth was alive to the song. The melody wove through the fog, caressing Ivor's ears, filling his mind with thoughts and feelings that were not his own. It was a music that seemed to speak to his soul, a song of longing and loss, of memories forgotten and truths untold. It was as if the unicorn's voice was singing of something ancient, something lost to time.

Ivor stepped forward, his legs trembling with awe, and the unicorn lowered its head, as though acknowledging his presence. The music stopped, but the air was thick with its lingering presence.

"You've come," the unicorn said, its voice a soft echo of the song. "Why?"

Ivor's throat was dry, and for a moment, he couldn't find his voice. "I... I heard the song," he said finally, his voice hoarse. "It called to me. I had to find it."

The unicorn tilted its head, its eyes studying him. "Why? What is it you seek in the song of a creature like me?"

Ivor felt a pang of uncertainty. He had been driven by a compulsion, an obsession to find the source of the melody. But now, standing in the presence of the creature, something deep inside him began to unravel. "I don't know," he admitted. "I thought... I thought it would bring me peace. Or understanding. Something I've been searching for my entire life."

The unicorn's eyes softened, and it took a slow step forward, its voice gentle. "The song you hear is not mine to give. It is an echo of the world itself, a melody sung by time and memory. It carries the weight of everything that has passed and everything that will come. And yet, you believe it will bring you peace. But peace is not something to be found outside of yourself."

Ivor's chest tightened, his mind struggling to comprehend. "But it's so beautiful," he said, his voice trembling. "The melody, the way it fills me... it feels like everything I've been searching for."

The unicorn nodded. "It is beautiful, yes. But beauty alone cannot heal what is broken inside. You think you seek the song, but what you are truly seeking is something deeper. It is not the sound that calls you, but the promise of what it represents—a promise of connection, of understanding, of belonging."

Ivor's heart ached at the words. He had spent his life searching for something, anything, that would fill the emptiness inside of him. He had thought the song, the unicorn, the magic of the mountains, would be the answer. But now, standing there, facing the truth of what the unicorn had said, he realized that the emptiness was not somcthing that could be fixed by external forces. He had been looking for peace in the wrong places.

The unicorn stepped closer, its presence warm and comforting. "You have already found the answer, Ivor. You were never meant to find peace through me. You must find it within yourself, in the way you live, the way you treat others, the way you embrace the world."

Ivor stared at the unicorn, feeling a weight lift from his chest. The emptiness he had felt for so long didn't need to be filled with something outside of him—it needed to be embraced, understood, and healed from within.

As the unicorn turned to leave, the melody began again, this time softer, more distant. But it wasn't the same haunting sound. It was no longer a call. It was a reminder. The song would continue, but now, it would not hold him captive. Ivor smiled softly, the peace he had sought for so long beginning to settle in his heart, a peace that would never come from an external source, but from within himself.

And with that realization, the world around him seemed to grow quieter, as though the mountains themselves had sighed in relief, content in the knowledge that Ivor had found the only thing he needed all along: himself.

# The Dark Unicorn

In the quiet, untouched valleys of the Eldwyn forest, there once roamed a unicorn named Auriel. His coat was as white as freshly fallen snow, his mane a cascade of silken silver that sparkled like the stars in the sky. His horn was sharp and luminous, a beacon of purity and grace. For centuries, he had been the guardian of the forest, a protector of its magic and its creatures. His presence brought peace, and his voice, when he spoke, was like the whisper of wind through the trees—gentle and soothing. He was a creature of light, a symbol of everything good and righteous in the world.

But that was before the shadows began to creep into his heart.

It had started slowly, like a shadow at dusk, barely noticeable at first. The first flicker of darkness had appeared on a night when Auriel had been particularly weary, burdened by the responsibility of protecting the forest. He had ventured too far from the heart of Eldwyn, into the mountains where the air was thin and the stars seemed to disappear behind thick clouds. There, in the stillness of the night, he had encountered a strange, hooded figure—a being whose eyes burned with an unnatural glow. The figure spoke to him in riddles, offering promises of power, of peace, and of an end to the endless solitude that had begun to haunt him.

At first, Auriel had refused. But the figure's words lingered in his mind, planting seeds of doubt, and when the darkness that surrounded him seemed to press harder against his heart, Auriel had given in. He accepted the stranger's offer, believing that the power to protect the forest would be greater if he could wield the dark forces he had been warned about. He didn't know what the consequences would be, but he was desperate to end his growing sense of emptiness.

The moment he agreed, the darkness surged through him like a violent storm. His body convulsed as shadows twisted around his form, and when he opened his eyes, his once-gleaming coat was now a deep, unsettling black. His mane, once bright as silver, now appeared like strands of ash, and his horn, once a beacon of light, was now jagged and menacing, dark tendrils crawling up its length. The pure magic he had once carried was tainted, turned into something cold and distant.

Auriel returned to the Eldwyn forest, but it was no longer the same. The trees no longer seemed to greet him with warmth, the creatures no longer regarded him with trust. The forest, once alive with the harmony of nature, now seemed to whisper in fear. The darkness had consumed him, and with it, the light he had once embodied.

As days passed, Auriel wandered aimlessly through the forest, feeling a deep, gnawing emptiness in his chest. He had destroyed the very thing he had loved most—his purity, his essence. And now, he felt nothing but regret, nothing but sorrow for the creature he had become.

He knew he had to find a way to restore what he had lost. He could no longer bear the weight of his own corruption. He had heard rumors of a place deep within the heart of the forest, a hidden glade where the oldest magic of the world was said to reside. It was a place untouched by time, where the forces of light and dark balanced in harmony, and where even the most tainted soul could find redemption.

With no other choice, Auriel set out in search of the glade. His journey was long, and the deeper he ventured into the forest, the stronger the pull of the darkness seemed to become. His once-gleaming hooves left marks of shadow wherever he stepped, and the creatures that once revered him now ran from him in terror. The magic that had once been his to command now seemed to mock him, turning every step into a painful reminder of the promise he had broken.

Finally, after what seemed like an eternity, Auriel found the glade. It was as beautiful as the legends had described—glowing flowers surrounded a clear pool of water, and the trees towered high above, their branches interwoven to form a protective canopy. The air was heavy with an ancient, calming magic that seemed to wrap around Auriel like a soft embrace. But even here, the darkness within him did not subside.

He approached the pool, gazing down at the reflection of the creature he had become. The unicorn that stared back at him was unrecognizable—a twisted shadow of the once-pure guardian. His eyes, once full of light, now reflected only sorrow and regret.

It was then that a voice, soft yet commanding, filled the glade. "You seek redemption, but you have already chosen your path."

Auriel spun around, his heart pounding in his chest. The voice belonged to a figure standing before him, a being of light whose presence filled the glade with warmth. It was a woman, tall and graceful, her hair flowing like golden rivers, her eyes filled with ancient wisdom.

"You cannot undo what has been done," she continued, her voice both soothing and firm. "You cannot simply erase the darkness you have embraced."

"I didn't mean for this to happen," Auriel whispered, his voice trembling with anguish. "I only wanted to protect the forest. I thought... I thought power would make me stronger, but it only consumed me."

The woman nodded, her gaze understanding but unwavering. "Power can protect, yes, but it can also destroy. You have learned the consequences of wielding power without understanding its true nature. You cannot restore your lost purity, for it was not taken from you—it was given away."

Auriel's heart sank. He had hoped for a way to turn back the clock, to reclaim the innocence he had lost. But the woman's words struck a hard truth—he could not simply undo what he had done. The darkness was part of him now, woven into the very fabric of his being.

"Then what am I supposed to do?" he asked, the despair in his voice evident.

The woman smiled softly, her expression gentle. "You must learn to live with the choices you've made. Redemption is not about erasing the past, but about learning to accept it, to grow from it. You must find balance within yourself—the light and the dark, working together, not in conflict."

As the woman spoke, Auriel felt a change within himself. It was subtle at first—a flicker of light within the darkness, a soft reminder of the purity that still resided within him, hidden beneath the shadow. He realized that redemption was not about returning to who he had been, but about accepting the duality within him and learning to use both the light and the dark for good.

With a deep breath, Auriel nodded. He would never be the same as he once was. But perhaps that was not the point. The path to redemption, he understood now, was not about perfection. It was about acceptance. And in that acceptance, he would find a new way to protect the forest—not through the purity of his past, but through the strength of his journey.

And with that realization, the darkness within him began to soften, the shadows lifting just enough to allow a sliver of light to shine through.

# The Unicorn's Island

The island of Virelia had long been forgotten by the world. Its location remained a secret, hidden beneath the clouds where the seas ran deep and the winds carried whispers of ancient magic. To the outside world, it was nothing more than a myth, a fragment of stories passed down through generations. But those who had been fortunate enough to set foot on its shores knew the truth—the island was real, and it was home to creatures of unimaginable beauty: the unicorns.

For centuries, the unicorns had lived in harmony with the island's natural wonders. They were not just animals; they were the island's guardians, the embodiment of its magic. Their horns shimmered like silver light, casting a glow that kept the land lush and vibrant. The flowers bloomed eternally, the trees grew tall and strong, and the rivers ran clear and pure, all thanks to the presence of the unicorns. In return, the unicorns thrived in a paradise that no one else could access.

But now, the island was dying.

The once-vibrant colors of Virelia had begun to fade, as if the very essence of the island had started to unravel. The unicorns grew weaker, their coats losing their luster, their magic slowly draining. The flowers wilted, the trees began to wither, and the rivers started to dry. Something had gone wrong, something ancient and unseen, and the unicorns could do nothing to stop it. They were the island's protectors, yet even their magic had its limits.

In the heart of the island stood a temple, an ancient structure that had long since fallen into disrepair. It was here that the unicorns gathered, seeking answers from the island's ancient magic. But it was not the unicorns who would restore the island's fading light—it would take a human. A brave soul who dared to venture into the heart of Virelia and face the unknown to save it.

That soul came in the form of Arianne, a young woman who had spent her life searching for the island of Virelia. Her grandmother had told her stories about it, speaking of the unicorns and the island's wondrous magic. Arianne had always believed that there was truth in those stories, that the island was real, and that the unicorns were not just creatures of myth. And now, with the island dying, Arianne knew she had to find it—she had to be the one to save it.

Arianne had grown up near the sea, and the ocean had always called to her. She spent years searching for the island, following the clues her grandmother had left behind, until one day, a storm led her to its shores. As the mist cleared, she saw it—a lush paradise rising from the sea, a place that felt like it had been carved from the dreams of the gods themselves.

She stepped onto the island, breathless at the beauty around her. The air was thick with the scent of salt and wildflowers, the ground soft beneath her feet. But as she ventured further into the heart of the island, she saw the signs of its fading life—the flowers had begun to droop, the trees stood like dying giants, and the once-glimmering rivers were little more than trickling streams.

It wasn't long before she encountered the unicorns. They stood in a clearing, their once-shining coats dull and tired, their eyes filled with sadness. Arianne approached them cautiously, her heart heavy with the knowledge that they were not the same as the stories she had heard.

One of the unicorns, an older mare with a coat of pale blue, stepped forward. Her horn glowed faintly, and her gaze was sharp, though her spirit seemed weary.

"You've come," the unicorn said, her voice soft yet strong, like the wind through the trees. "You are the one chosen to restore the island. You are the last hope."

Arianne's heart fluttered in her chest. "What happened? What's causing the island to fade?"

The unicorn lowered her head, her eyes sorrowful. "Long ago, we made a pact with the forces of nature. In exchange for our protection, the island was granted eternal life. But now, the balance has shifted. A darkness has crept into the heart of the island, and it is feeding on the magic we once shared. We have no power left to fight it."

Arianne's brow furrowed with concern. "And how can I help? What must I do?"

The unicorn's horn shimmered brighter. "You must journey to the temple, to the very heart of Virelia. There, you will find the source of the darkness. But be warned: the path is not an easy one. You will face trials, and the darkness will try to deceive you. It will prey on your fears and your doubts. But only by facing it head-on can you hope to restore the island's magic."

With no time to waste, Arianne set off toward the temple. The journey was long and treacherous, the path winding through dense forests and across barren hills. The air seemed heavier as she approached the temple, the very ground beneath her feet feeling like it was sinking into shadow. She could feel the darkness growing stronger with every step.

When she finally reached the temple, it stood before her like a monument to a forgotten time. The stone walls were cracked and worn, the carvings faded by centuries of neglect. Inside, the temple was cold, the air thick with an oppressive energy. In the center of the room stood an altar, where a dark crystal pulsed with an eerie, unnatural light.

As Arianne approached the altar, she felt the weight of the darkness pressing against her, suffocating her thoughts. The crystal before her seemed to draw in the light around it, casting the room into deeper shadows. But in the midst of it all, Arianne realized something—the darkness was not an external force. It was within her, feeding on her doubts, her fears, the parts of herself she had long ignored.

The lesson became clear: the island's decay, the fading of the unicorns' magic, was a reflection of her own inner turmoil. The darkness had grown because she had let it. The power to restore the island did not lie in some external force—it lay in her own willingness to confront the darkness inside her.

With trembling hands, Arianne reached out and touched the crystal. She let the darkness flood through her, embracing it, acknowledging it. It was a part of her, just as the light was. The two could not exist without the other. In that moment, Arianne understood: balance, not perfection, was the key to healing.

The crystal shattered, and a wave of light erupted from it, flooding the temple. The shadows retreated, and the temple's walls seemed to breathe once more. Outside, the island began to glow with life again. The trees stood tall, the flowers bloomed, and the rivers flowed clear and pure.

The unicorns gathered around Arianne as the island's magic restored itself. Their coats gleamed with renewed brilliance, and their eyes were filled with gratitude. Arianne smiled, knowing that the island was saved—not by brute strength, but by the courage to face her own darkness.

As she stood there, surrounded by the beauty of the reborn island, Arianne realized the true lesson of her journey: only by accepting both light and shadow within herself could she truly restore the balance of the world. And in that balance, the magic of Virelia would live on, as long as she remembered that it was within her, always.

# The Unicorn's Eternal Love

In the heart of the Enchanted Forest, nestled deep within the verdant hills and hidden from the eyes of the world, lived two unicorns—Eldrin and Serenna. They were ancient beings, whose coats shimmered like moonlight on still water, and their horns spiraled with magic older than the earth itself. For centuries, they had roamed the forest together, bound by a love that transcended time. They had witnessed the rise and fall of kingdoms, the shifting of seasons, and the slow passage of millennia. Their bond was unbreakable, a force that had weathered every storm, every trial, every moment of darkness.

But now, their love was to be tested in a way it had never been before.

One quiet evening, as the two unicorns stood together beneath the ancient oak tree in the heart of the forest, a figure appeared—a being cloaked in dark, shifting shadows. The figure's presence was unsettling, and even the wind seemed to hold its breath as it approached them.

"I come on behalf of the Elder Council," the figure said, its voice a low murmur that sent a chill through the air. "There is a final test you must face, a test to prove that your bond is as eternal as you claim it to be."

Eldrin and Serenna exchanged glances, their hearts already sensing that this was no ordinary trial. Their love had always been their greatest strength, but they knew that nothing in the magical realms was ever given without a price.

"What is this test?" Serenna asked, her voice calm yet edged with concern.

The figure's eyes glimmered from beneath its hood, a flicker of something ancient in their depths. "You will be separated. For one year, you will live apart. You will face your own fears, your own vulnerabilities, without the support of the other. Only when the year has passed will you be allowed to reunite. If your bond is true, it will survive this separation. If not, then it will fade, and you will both be lost to the ages."

The air grew heavy with silence. Eldrin's heart thundered in his chest, and Serenna's gaze softened with sadness. They had never been apart for more than a moment, their connection so deep that it felt like an extension of their very souls. The thought of living without her was unbearable, yet neither could deny that the challenge before them was one they could not refuse. It was a test not just of their love, but of their very essence.

"One year," Eldrin whispered, his voice filled with an unspoken promise. "We will endure this. Together."

Serenna nodded, her eyes bright with unshed tears. "If our love is true, it will survive."

And so, without another word, the figure waved its hand, and the forest around them seemed to shimmer, as though the very fabric of time had split in two. The world around them shifted, the trees growing taller, the sky darkening as if to mark the beginning of their separation.

The year began.

Eldrin wandered through the forest, his heart heavy with grief. The wind no longer felt the same without Serenna by his side, and the magic that had always flowed so freely now felt distant and cold. Every day, he felt the absence of her laughter, the warmth of her presence, like a void within him. The forest, once vibrant with life, now seemed eerily quiet, as though it too mourned the loss of their bond.

Serenna, too, felt the weight of their separation. Though the forest was still beautiful, it had lost its brightness without Eldrin's light beside her. Every moment of solitude was a reminder of the love she missed, the connection that had defined her existence for so long. Yet, as the days turned to weeks, and the weeks to months, she began to notice something strange. The isolation that once felt suffocating now gave her space to reflect, to discover parts of herself she had long overlooked.

She found that her magic, though diminished in her loneliness, was still present. It was quieter, more introspective, but it was still there. She realized that her love for Eldrin was not the sole thing that defined her. There was a strength within her, a resilience she had never known until now.

And so, the year passed.

When the time finally arrived for them to reunite, Eldrin and Serenna met once more beneath the ancient oak tree, where their journey had begun. The first sight of each other made their hearts ache with longing, but there was something different now. They had both changed, and though their love had survived, it had grown deeper, more complex. It was no longer the love of two beings who were inseparable; it was the love of two individuals who had learned to stand on their own, even when apart.

As they gazed into each other's eyes, the magic of the forest swirled around them, rekindling the bond that had been tested. But it was not just the magic of the forest that brought them back together—it was the understanding that had bloomed in their time apart. They had both faced their own fears, their own vulnerabilities, and come to understand that their love was not about dependency, but about balance. The strength of their love did not lie in never being apart, but in knowing that even when separated, they could still carry each other in their hearts.

The figure from the Elder Council reappeared, watching them silently. "You have passed the test," it said, its voice softer now. "Your bond is stronger than ever, not because you are never apart, but because you have learned to love yourselves fully, as well as each other."

Eldrin and Serenna stood together, their horns glowing with a soft, radiant light. They had learned that true love was not about clinging to one another, but about supporting each other's growth, understanding that the connection between them would always be there, even in moments of distance.

As they walked side by side, the forest around them began to blossom once more. The trees stood taller, the flowers bloomed in brilliant hues, and the air filled with the song of birds returning to their nests. The island, once again alive with their love, had been restored—not just by the magic they wielded, but by the strength of their hearts.

And in that moment, they understood the true meaning of their bond. Love, they had learned, was not about possession or permanence; it was about trust, growth, and the ability to stand together, no matter the distance between them.

# Unicorn's Shadow

Serena, the unicorn of the Enchanted Meadows, had always been proud of the bond between herself and her shadow. It was a part of her, a reflection of the grace and magic that ran through her veins. From the moment she first took form, her shadow had danced alongside her, mimicking her every movement, always a steady presence. No matter how far she traveled, no matter how much the winds howled or the sun blazed down, the shadow remained steadfast. It had become a symbol of her strength and identity.

But one morning, as the first light of dawn touched the meadow, Serena noticed something strange. As she stood on the grass, basking in the warmth of the rising sun, her shadow was missing.

She blinked, confused, and then looked down again. No dark form stretched behind her, no cool silhouette to match the soft glow of her white coat. A wave of unease washed over her, a sensation unfamiliar to the usually calm and resolute unicorn.

She stood still, her hooves rooted in the earth, trying to make sense of what had happened. She turned around, expecting to see the shadow lingering behind her. But there was nothing. The meadow, once alive with the gentle rhythm of morning, seemed to hold its breath as she moved through it. She reached out to the trees, to the flowers, seeking answers, but the world around her remained silent.

In that moment, a deep sense of loss settled within Serena's chest. Her shadow was not just a companion—it was a reflection of who she was. Without it, she felt incomplete, as though a part of herself had vanished into the ether. The warmth of the sun on her back no longer felt the same, and the wind, once invigorating, now felt hollow.

Determined to restore what was lost, Serena set off on a journey. She ventured deep into the heart of the Enchanted Meadows, where the air thickened with magic, hoping to find answers in the mysterious lands that stretched far beyond her usual territory. Her steps were swift, but the landscape seemed unfamiliar, as though it too had shifted in her absence. The usual vibrant flowers were wilting, the trees that once hummed with ancient power were silent.

Days passed, and the further Serena went, the more the land seemed to change. The once bright skies grew dimmer, the air heavier. She encountered creatures who whispered in hushed tones, their eyes wide with fear. None of them spoke of shadows, but they all seemed to know that something had shifted. Finally, after what felt like weeks, Serena stumbled upon an old, forgotten path that led into a dense forest—a place she had never dared to enter.

The trees here were twisted, their bark blackened, their leaves rustling with a sound that was both eerie and familiar. The air grew thick, as if something unseen watched her every move. Serena continued forward, her heart pounding as her hooves clicked softly against the dry, brittle leaves beneath her. She knew she was close to something important, though she couldn't quite grasp what it was.

At the center of the forest, hidden beneath a veil of shadows, she found a clearing bathed in the soft light of a pale moon. In the center of the clearing stood a stone pedestal, cracked and weathered, but still standing strong. Upon the pedestal lay her shadow.

But this was not the shadow she had known. It was no longer a mere reflection of herself. It was a shifting form, full of swirling colors and depths she had never seen. The shadow had taken on a life of its own, moving with fluid grace, not bound to her body as it had been before.

Serena approached cautiously, her heart beating faster as she neared the pedestal. The shadow seemed to notice her, swirling in the air, taking shape and form. It was as if it was calling to her, beckoning her to understand something deeper, something hidden within herself.

"Why did you leave me?" Serena whispered, her voice full of grief. She reached out a trembling hoof, the tips of her fur brushing against the shadow's shifting form. "Why did you disappear?"

The shadow shimmered, as though trying to communicate, but no words came. Instead, Serena felt a strange pull inside her—a warmth in her chest, a deep ache that stretched into her very soul. It was then that the realization hit her like a wave: her shadow had not simply disappeared. It had separated itself, seeking something she had refused to face.

The shadow had become a mirror, a reflection not just of her light, but of her darkness, her fears, and the parts of herself she had hidden for so long. Serena had always been proud of her strength, her purity, but in doing so, she had neglected the darker parts of herself—the self-doubt, the loneliness, the fragility that she had never allowed to surface. The shadow had left, not because it had chosen to, but because she had pushed it away.

Tears welled up in Serena's eyes as she understood the truth. The shadow was not just a companion; it was a part of her soul, a balance between light and darkness. By denying it, she had denied a crucial part of herself.

In that moment, Serena did something she had never done before. She let go of her pride and her fear. She allowed herself to accept the darkness that had always been with her, to acknowledge the parts of herself she had kept hidden. As she did, the shadow began to glow with a soft, golden light, returning to its original form.

The shadow drifted back to Serena, embracing her like an old friend, settling once more against her body, but with a new depth, a new understanding. The balance between light and dark was no longer a force to be feared—it was a part of her, a vital part of who she was.

The moment the shadow reunited with her, the world around Serena shifted. The trees in the forest began to hum, the air lightened, and the flowers around her bloomed once again. The Enchanted Meadows were alive with magic once more. The shadow had not only restored her sense of self—it had restored the world around her.

Serena stood in the clearing, feeling a newfound peace settle over her. She realized that, like her shadow, she was not just one thing. She was a combination of light and dark, joy and sorrow, strength and vulnerability. It was in accepting both sides of herself that she found true harmony.

As she turned to leave the forest, her shadow now fully restored, Serena smiled. She understood that sometimes, the parts of ourselves we fear the most are the ones that hold the greatest power. And by embracing them, we are made whole.

# The Moonlit Unicorn

Beneath the pale glow of a full moon, in a meadow surrounded by ancient, towering trees, a unicorn was born. Her coat shimmered with a silver-blue sheen, like the sky just before dawn, and her horn gleamed with the intensity of starlight. The night itself seemed to hold its breath as she took her first steps, the world whispering in reverence to the creature of legend that had appeared in the silence of the dark.

Liora, the Moonlit Unicorn, was unlike any unicorn the world had ever known. Her powers were not the simple magic of her kin—her horn could heal, her hooves could summon the rains, and her presence brought peace. But there was something more. Something deep within her, an untapped force that only the moon could reveal.

She grew up in the meadows of the Dreamwood Forest, a place where the trees whispered ancient secrets and the winds sang melodies of forgotten times. Liora's parents, gentle and wise, were the guardians of the forest, ensuring that its magic remained strong and pure. They loved their daughter dearly but were wary of the strange aura she carried. From the moment she was born, they knew that Liora was destined for something far greater than even they could comprehend.

As Liora matured, she began to understand the weight of her heritage. Her magic, while still young, pulsed with an intensity that sometimes frightened her. On nights when the moon hung high and full, she would feel an almost unbearable pull in her chest, as though something in her was straining to break free. She had learned to control the simpler aspects of her abilities—summoning a breeze to cool the air, or coaxing flowers to bloom in the barren soil—but the deeper magic, the one tied to the very heart of the moon itself, remained a mystery.

Her parents spoke of the ancient prophecy, one that foretold a unicorn born under the moon's light, whose magic would one day either save or destroy the world. They had warned Liora of the dangers of her power, telling her that only when she learned to control it would she be able to choose her destiny. But control was not something Liora understood. Her power surged through her veins with every heartbeat, and sometimes, it overwhelmed her.

One evening, as the full moon rose high above the Dreamwood, a storm began to stir in the distance. Liora felt it first—an unnatural wind, sharp and cold, sweeping through the forest. The trees groaned under its force, and the sky darkened in ways that felt unnatural. Liora stood at the edge of the meadow, her eyes fixed on the darkening horizon. She could feel it—something was coming. Something she was meant to face.

As the wind howled louder, a figure emerged from the forest—a tall man cloaked in shadows. His eyes gleamed with a strange light, and his presence seemed to absorb the very energy of the night. Liora's heart pounded in her chest as she stepped forward, the air around her shimmering with magic. The man stopped before her, his eyes locking with hers.

"You are the one, aren't you?" he asked, his voice low and full of dark power. "The Moonlit Unicorn, born to decide the fate of the world."

Liora didn't answer. She felt the power within her begin to stir, as if her very essence was reaching out to meet his.

"I am," she said finally, her voice steady despite the fear in her heart. "But I don't understand the prophecy. I don't understand why I was born with this magic, or what I'm supposed to do with it."

The man smiled, a cold, calculating smile. "The moon's magic is both a gift and a curse. You have the power to restore balance to the world, or to destroy it. You must choose."

The words hung in the air like a weight, and Liora felt the pull of her power surge again, stronger this time. She could feel it—the ancient magic of the moon, calling to her. It wanted to break free, wanted to be unleashed. She could feel it in her veins, in the depths of her soul.

The man stepped closer, his eyes glowing brighter. "I seek to control this power, to use it for my own purposes. Join me, and we can reshape the world as we see fit. Together, we can wield the moon's magic, control it, and make everything bow to our will."

Liora's heart raced as the power within her surged once more, threatening to break free. But this time, something inside her shifted. She could feel the presence of the moon, a constant, patient force, urging her to look within herself, to find the true source of her power. She knew then that the man's promises of control were empty. He didn't understand the moon's magic. It wasn't meant to be wielded, controlled, or bent to someone's will—it was meant to guide, to flow through the world, a force that connected all living things.

"No," she said, her voice clear and firm. "I will not let you use this power for destruction."

The man's eyes flashed with anger, and he reached out, his hands crackling with dark energy. "Then you will fall, as all who defy me do."

In that moment, Liora knew what she had to do. She closed her eyes, letting the power surge through her. She did not fight it; instead, she embraced it. She let it fill her, let it connect her to the moon, to the forest, to everything that was alive. Her horn glowed brighter than ever before, a beam of pure moonlight piercing the storm around them.

The man recoiled as the light surrounded him, a powerful force that he could not control. Liora's magic was not one of domination, but of balance. She didn't fight him with the intent to destroy him; she simply let the moon's magic do what it was meant to do—restore the harmony of the world.

The storm ceased, the clouds parted, and the moonlight bathed the meadow in a soft, peaceful glow. The man, his power drained, fell to the ground, vanquished by the force of Liora's magic. But Liora stood tall, her heart calm now, knowing that her power had not been used for control or conquest—but for balance.

As the night settled, the world around her seemed to breathe again. The trees, the flowers, the animals of the forest—everything was in harmony. And Liora, the Moonlit Unicorn, understood at last. Her power was not to be feared or hidden. It was to be embraced, used only to restore what had been lost, to heal what had been broken. The moon had never been about domination—it had always been about connection.

And in that moment, Liora finally understood that she wasn't just a creature born under the moon's light—she was the embodiment of it, a reminder that true power lies not in control, but in the ability to live in harmony with the world around us.

# The Thief and the Unicorn

Rafe had always been a master of his craft—a clever, nimble thief with a reputation that stretched across kingdoms. His fingers were quick, his mind sharper, and his heart colder than the steel he carried in his belt. He didn't steal for greed, but for the thrill of it. The challenge. He sought out the rarest, most impossible prizes and relished in the game. He had stolen jewels that could buy kingdoms, artifacts from ancient temples, and gold from the vaults of kings. But there was one prize that had always eluded him—the unicorn's horn.

Legends whispered of its power: the horn could heal wounds, cure sickness, and grant wishes to those who were worthy. It was said to hold magic older than the world itself, and no thief had ever successfully claimed it. Many had tried, but the unicorns were elusive, and the creatures were protected by their ancient magic. But Rafe was not one to shy away from a challenge, especially one that had so many potential rewards.

It took him months to track the unicorn. He studied the forest, read ancient scrolls, and watched the stars for clues. He learned its patterns, its movements, its habits. The unicorn was not as untouchable as the stories suggested. All creatures had a weakness, and Rafe knew how to exploit it.

On the night he finally made his move, the moon was high and full, casting a pale glow over the meadows where the unicorn grazed. Rafe had prepared for this night for weeks, crafting the perfect plan. His footsteps were soundless on the grass as he crept closer to the creature, whose glowing coat illuminated the darkness like a beacon. Its long, silvery mane shimmered as it bent its head to nibble on the dew-covered grass. The horn, twisting upward like a spiral of light, was exactly as he had imagined it—perfect, majestic, and impossibly beautiful.

Rafe knew that this was his moment. The unicorn had always been vigilant, but tonight, the magic seemed to be at rest, its guard lowered. He approached, moving silently, a small dagger in his hand. He had no intention of harming the creature, but he needed to sever the horn, just enough to claim his prize. A swift, precise cut, and he would have what every thief in history had failed to obtain.

As his hand reached for the unicorn's horn, the creature's head jerked up, its ears flicking. It was faster than he had anticipated, and before he could react, the unicorn turned to face him. Its eyes were pools of liquid silver, sharp and intelligent, and in that moment, Rafe realized his mistake.

"You should not have come," the unicorn's voice was clear, though its lips did not move. The words rang in his mind, a soft echo in the stillness of the night.

Rafe froze. He had been prepared for resistance, but not for speech. The unicorn's magic was palpable, thick in the air like a hum. The ground beneath his feet seemed to shift, as though the earth itself was aware of his intrusion.

"I've come for your horn," Rafe said, trying to sound confident, though the certainty in his voice faltered under the weight of the creature's gaze. "I've heard of its power. I can't leave without it."

The unicorn tilted its head, its silver mane catching the light. "The horn is not a trinket for greed. It is not a trophy to be claimed."

"I don't seek wealth or power," Rafe replied, his voice steadying. "I need it for a good cause. To save someone I care about. Please... let me take it."

The unicorn's eyes softened, its expression almost pitying. "You seek to take what does not belong to you. You think you can wield power, but you do not understand the cost."

Rafe's hand tightened around the dagger. "What cost? What could possibly be worse than losing someone I love?"

The unicorn moved closer, its presence overwhelming. "The cost is your soul. The cost is the magic within you, which you will never get back once you steal it."

Rafe hesitated, the words weighing heavily on him. He had been trained to ignore the moral questions that arose with every theft. It was part of the job, the game. But here, in the presence of the unicorn, the rules were different. The creature's gaze pierced him like a blade, cutting through the hardened exterior he had spent years building.

"I don't want to harm you," Rafe said, his voice softer now, almost a whisper. "But I can't turn back."

The unicorn nodded slowly, as if it had been expecting this answer. "Then you must face the consequences, as we all must. But know this: the price of magic is not just your soul—it is your ability to truly love."

Before Rafe could react, the unicorn stepped forward, its horn glowing with an ethereal light. A sharp, piercing pain shot through his chest, unlike anything he had ever felt. It wasn't physical—it was something deeper, a loss that tore through him, unraveling the very fabric of his being. The world spun around him, and in a moment of blinding clarity, he saw it—the truth of the unicorn's words.

The magic that the horn held was not to be taken for granted. It was a reminder of the purity that Rafe had long abandoned. The bond that came with true love, with true connection, was more valuable than any prize he could ever steal.

When the light faded, Rafe fell to his knees, gasping for breath. The dagger slipped from his hand, forgotten. The unicorn stood before him, no longer a threat but a presence of profound understanding.

"I didn't mean to," Rafe murmured, his voice raw. "I never meant to lose myself."

The unicorn's eyes softened. "You didn't lose yourself, thief. You never had yourself to begin with. But you can choose to change now. You can choose to let go of the greed and find something real."

Rafe looked up, his heart aching, not from the pain, but from the realization that everything he had stolen, everything he had built, had been a lie. The true magic wasn't in the taking—it was in the giving, the understanding, and the connection he had denied for so long.

The unicorn turned to leave, its hooves light on the ground. "You are free, thief. You have the choice to change, to find what you truly seek."

Rafe remained where he was, the weight of the world pressing on him. The unicorn's horn was still a distant dream, but for the first time, he understood that there was something far greater than magic—there was the power of redemption, the chance to rebuild what had been broken.

And as the moonlight bathed the meadow in a soft glow, Rafe realized that the greatest prize was not the horn he had sought, but the chance to reclaim the love and life he had long since abandoned.

# The Silent Unicorn

In the heart of the sprawling Eldenwood Forest, beneath the towering trees that whispered of ancient times, there lived a unicorn named Seraphina. She was as beautiful as the moonlit sky, her coat gleaming silver and her horn a spiral of light that shimmered even in the darkest night. She was known throughout the forest for her gentle nature and the grace with which she moved, but there was something different about her that others could not quite place—she was silent.

Seraphina had never spoken a word. No one knew why. Some believed that a curse had been placed upon her at birth, others whispered that her voice was stolen by a dark force. But the truth was much simpler—she had never needed to speak. In a world where words flowed easily from the mouths of creatures large and small, Seraphina had learned to communicate without them. She spoke in gestures, in the way she carried herself, in the soft, melodic hums that sometimes escaped her as she moved through the forest. The creatures of Eldenwood understood her without words. She had become a part of the forest's silent rhythm, a being whose presence was enough.

But one day, the balance of the forest was shattered. A terrible blight swept through Eldenwood, a sickness that drained the life from the trees, leaving them withered and dry. The rivers, once sparkling with crystal-clear water, turned murky and foul. Animals that had always lived in harmony with the land began to flee, unable to bear the heavy air that hung over the forest. The wind, which once sang through the leaves, was now a mournful sigh, carrying the stench of decay.

Seraphina could feel the pain in the very roots of the earth. Her heart, so in tune with the forest, ached with every passing moment. But she was powerless. She had no words to comfort the creatures who came to her in desperation, no voice to call upon the ancient magic that had once protected Eldenwood. The silent unicorn could only watch as the life around her drained away.

One day, as Seraphina wandered deeper into the blighted part of the forest, she came upon a clearing where an old owl perched upon a twisted branch. His feathers were dull, his eyes sunken with the weight of sorrow. He had been one of the forest's wisest creatures, known for his ability to guide those who sought wisdom. But now, his gaze was empty, and his body seemed frail, the magic of Eldenwood retreating from him as well.

"Seraphina," the owl croaked, his voice raspy and faint. "What will we do? The forest is dying, and you—our last hope—cannot speak. You have no words to save us."

Seraphina stood before him, her heart heavy with the weight of his words. She wanted to reply, to reassure him that she would find a way, but her silence was all that remained. The owl's words stung, for in that moment, Seraphina realized something painful: her silence had always been her strength, but now it felt like her greatest weakness. She could no longer communicate as she once had. The creatures of Eldenwood were desperate, and they needed more than gestures, more than soft hums. They needed someone who could speak, who could rally the magic of the forest and guide them to salvation.

But Seraphina refused to give in to despair. If she could not speak, she would find another way. She closed her eyes and focused on the deepest part of her being, where her magic lay dormant, waiting. She had always known that words were not the only way to communicate—magic itself could be a language, a force that spoke in ways far beyond speech.

With a gentle step forward, Seraphina lowered her horn to the earth. The forest seemed to hold its breath as her magic surged through the ground, a quiet current that vibrated through the soil. The trees responded, their withered branches stirring as if awakening from a long slumber. The rivers, though still murky, rippled as the life force of the earth began to pulse again. The owl blinked in surprise, his eyes widening as the clearing around them shifted.

For the first time in what felt like an eternity, Seraphina felt the power within her align with the world around her. She had always been connected to the land, but now, in this moment of silent determination, she found a new way to communicate with it—through the magic she had long kept hidden, the power that had always been there, waiting for her to understand.

As the magic rippled outward, Seraphina felt a shift in the air. The blight that had poisoned the forest began to lift, ever so slowly, like the first rays of sunlight breaking through the clouds after a storm. The trees began to regain their strength, their leaves trembling with new life. The animals, sensing the change, began to return, their bodies no longer weak from hunger or fear.

The owl, now standing tall, looked at Seraphina with wonder. "You have done it," he said, his voice no longer faint but strong with the power of the forest. "You have saved us, not with words, but with your spirit. You have spoken in the language of magic, the language that binds all life together."

Seraphina felt a warmth in her chest, a lightness that came from within. She realized now that her silence had not been a curse. It had been her greatest strength. Her magic, her connection to the world, had always been deeper than words. It was not her ability to speak that made her powerful—it was her ability to listen. To listen to the world around her, to the creatures of Eldenwood, to the earth beneath her hooves. And in that listening, she had found a way to heal what was broken.

The forest, once again alive with magic, seemed to breathe with a new rhythm. Seraphina stood at its heart, her body glowing with the quiet power that came from understanding. She had found her voice not in words, but in the stillness that allowed her to truly hear.

And in the end, Seraphina understood that silence, when embraced, could speak louder than any words ever could. The magic of the world did not need to be spoken—it needed to be felt, in the heart, in the soul, and in the quiet moments when we listen deeply enough to hear it.

# The Unicorn and the Enchanted Book

In the heart of the Verdant Valley, where the trees towered like ancient guardians and the rivers ran with liquid crystal, there lived a unicorn named Elara. She had lived for centuries, her silver coat gleaming like moonlight on still waters, and her horn, a twisted spiral of purest white, was a symbol of the old magic that coursed through the world. But despite her age, Elara had always felt a deep sense of longing. She knew she was not like other creatures of the valley. There was a purpose to her existence, a reason for the magic that flowed through her veins, but it had always eluded her. Her parents, guardians of the valley and ancient keepers of its secrets, had always told her that one day, she would understand her true purpose. But that day had never come.

One crisp autumn evening, as the sun dipped below the horizon and the first stars twinkled in the sky, Elara wandered farther than usual. Her hooves clicked softly against the moss-covered earth as she made her way through the dense forest. The air was thick with the scent of pine and earth, but there was something else in the wind—a sense of something ancient, something calling to her.

The pull was undeniable, a soft whisper in her heart, urging her to follow. She threaded her way through the trees until she reached the base of a great, old oak, its roots twisting out of the earth like ancient serpents. There, at the foot of the tree, half-buried in the soft soil, was a book. Its cover was unlike anything Elara had ever seen—wrought in gold and silver, with intricate runes etched into the surface. The moment her eyes touched it, a surge of energy ran through her, a recognition deep in her soul.

Elara lowered her head and gently nudged the book with her horn, the old magic humming to life. The book opened without a sound, its pages glowing faintly in the twilight. As she began to read, the words shifted and changed, as if the book itself was alive, adjusting to her understanding. She had always been a quick learner, but this—it felt different. The words were ancient, speaking of a time long past, of the first unicorns and the magic that had given birth to them. But there, at the very heart of the book, was a revelation that stopped Elara cold.

It spoke of her—her lineage, her true purpose. She was not simply a guardian of the valley, as she had always assumed. She was the last of a line of unicorns chosen to restore balance to the world, to awaken the ancient magic that had long been dormant. Her horn was not just a tool of healing and light; it was the key to unlocking the old powers that had been sealed away for centuries. And in her, the magic of the unicorns had reached its fullest potential.

The realization hit Elara like a thunderbolt. She had always felt different, like a piece of herself was missing, like she had been waiting for something. Now she knew what it was. But there was a catch. The book also warned that the magic she carried was both a gift and a curse. She had been chosen, yes, but with the weight of that choice came a responsibility that no one—least of all Elara—could truly understand until the moment arrived. The book spoke of darkness, a force that sought to destroy the balance of the world, and that only she could stop it. But in doing so, she would have to sacrifice something vital—something that had always been part of her.

Elara's heart ached as she read those final words. The decision before her was clear: embrace her destiny and risk losing herself, or turn away and let the world continue its slow descent into chaos. But as she sat there, the weight of the decision pressing on her chest, something stirred deep within her. The valley, the creatures that lived there, the magic that had always been a part of her—none of it was truly separate from her. The world was part of her, and she was part of it. She could not simply walk away.

But the sacrifice—the loss—it gnawed at her. What would she have to give up to restore balance? Her magic, her freedom, or something deeper? As the stars began to fill the sky, a sense of peace settled over her. The answer was not in the book, not in the magic. The answer lay in the choice she made, in how she decided to shape the world around her.

The next morning, Elara set off toward the heart of the valley, the book still clutched in her hooves. She had made her decision. She would take up her mantle, fulfill her purpose, and face whatever came with courage. But she would not do it alone. She was not the last unicorn, and the magic of the world did not rest solely upon her shoulders. She had her friends, the creatures of the valley, the forest, the rivers—all of them had a role to play in the restoration of balance.

The journey would be difficult, and the path unclear, but as Elara walked through the golden morning light, she realized that the true cost of her destiny was not in what she had to give up, but in how she chose to move forward. The magic had always been hers, but now she understood its true power. It was not just in her horn or her bloodline. It was in her heart, her connection to the world around her, and the choices she made in every moment.

As the wind rustled the leaves above her, Elara felt the book's presence fade from her mind, the answers no longer so important. She had become her own story, her own legend. And in that, she understood what the book had never told her—sometimes the greatest magic comes not from ancient powers or prophecies, but from the willingness to embrace the unknown and trust in oneself.

And so, with a steady heart and a spirit that shone brighter than any star, Elara began the next chapter of her journey—not as a savior, but as a part of something much greater, something that could never truly be captured in a book.

# Unicorn in the Wild

For the first time in his life, Kiran felt the wind against his coat without the barrier of stone walls or iron fences. He had never known freedom—never known the untamed vastness of the world outside the small, confined space where he had been raised. For as long as he could remember, he had been kept in a cage of comfort, in a sanctuary where everything had been provided for him. His coat, a shimmering shade of pearly white, gleamed under the sun's tender gaze, and his long, spiraling horn was admired by all who visited. He had been raised with gentle hands and soothing words, taught that his existence was a gift to be cherished, to be adored. But all the while, something inside him had felt... restricted.

Now, as he stepped out into the open air for the first time, Kiran felt both exhilarated and terrified. The world was vast. The ground beneath his hooves felt different from the soft, manicured grass of the sanctuary; it was rough, uneven, full of unknown textures. The trees loomed large around him, and the sky stretched endlessly above him. His ears twitched nervously, attuned to every rustling leaf, every distant cry of an animal, every unfamiliar sound. For the first time, he was alone, truly alone, with no caretakers, no comforts.

The first few days were overwhelming. Kiran wandered through the forest, finding the food he needed—wild grasses, the occasional fruit hanging from the trees. But nothing came easily. The serenity he had been accustomed to now seemed like a distant memory. He had to learn to avoid predators, the jagged rocks that threatened to injure his soft hooves, and the biting insects that clung to his coat. Every step felt like a challenge, each moment an encounter with something unknown. He had been pampered, raised in a bubble, and now, the bubble had burst.

Kiran's heart began to sink with the weight of his own inadequacy. The freedom he had so longed for felt more like a burden now. There were no familiar faces, no soft voices calling him back to safety. He had to trust his instincts, something he had never fully learned to do. The world outside was harsh and indifferent, and Kiran felt like a child fumbling through a dark room, his once-illuminated path now swallowed by shadows.

One day, as Kiran moved deeper into the forest, he encountered something that terrified him. A pack of wild wolves, their eyes glowing in the dimming light, their teeth sharp and glistening. They circled him slowly, their growls low and menacing. He felt the cold weight of fear settle in his chest. He could not fight them; he had no experience in combat. His horn was a tool of magic, not a weapon of defense. The wolves seemed to sense his vulnerability, their slow steps predatory.

Just as the wolves closed in, something inside Kiran stirred—a sharp instinct, a force of nature that rose within him like a surge of electricity. His horn began to glow, not with the gentle light of his past, but with the fiery brilliance of his true power. Without thinking, he thrust his horn forward, unleashing a pulse of energy so powerful that it scattered the wolves, sending them fleeing into the shadows.

Kiran stood trembling, his heart racing in his chest. He had never known his magic could do that. For the first time in his life, he realized the depths of his power, the strength that had always been within him, waiting to be awakened. He had always relied on others to protect him, to guide him, but now, he understood that he was capable of more than he had ever imagined.

As the days passed, Kiran began to grow more confident. He learned to navigate the forest with more ease, to recognize the signs of danger and adapt. He discovered the rhythms of the world around him, the pulse of the earth beneath his hooves, the whispers of the wind in the trees. Slowly but surely, the wild began to feel less threatening and more like a home. He found peace in the solitude, a sense of belonging in the untamed beauty of the world.

One evening, as the sun dipped low and the sky turned a deep shade of crimson, Kiran stood on a hill, watching the horizon stretch before him. For the first time since his release, he felt truly free, not just in body, but in spirit. He had faced his fears, had overcome the limitations he had once placed on himself. The world was no longer a frightening place—it was his to explore, to understand, to live within. He no longer relied on the structure of his old life; he had built a new one for himself, shaped by his choices and his strength.

But then, as he turned to make his way deeper into the forest, he was stopped by a voice—a soft, melodic voice that seemed to drift on the wind. "Are you not afraid anymore?" it asked, gentle and knowing.

Kiran's heart skipped a beat. He turned to see a figure standing at the edge of the clearing—a figure with glowing eyes, a presence so calm and assured that Kiran felt an immediate connection. It was a fellow unicorn, one with a coat the color of twilight and a horn that shimmered like the stars.

"I was afraid," Kiran said, his voice steady but carrying the weight of all the days of doubt. "But I have learned something. The wild... it is not my enemy. It is my teacher."

The other unicorn nodded, a smile gracing their lips. "The wild is not meant to tame you, Kiran. It is meant to set you free. You were never meant to stay in captivity. You were always meant to discover the power that lies within you."

For a moment, Kiran felt a deep connection to the unicorn before him, as if their words were a mirror reflecting everything he had just realized. He had spent his life seeking safety, comfort, and answers. But the world, the wild world, had offered him something far more valuable: the chance to find himself.

As the two unicorns stood there, looking out at the vast expanse of the forest, Kiran understood. It was not the world that had changed. It was him. He was no longer the young, frightened creature in captivity. He was part of the wild, part of the endless cycle of life that thrived in every corner of the world. And that, more than anything, was the freedom he had been searching for.

He smiled, his heart full, knowing that his journey had only just begun.

# The Golden Unicorn

Every hundred years, the stars align in a way that whispers through the forests, across the plains, and deep into the hearts of those who still believe in magic. It is a rare and wondrous event, one that brings with it the appearance of a creature of pure legend: the Golden Unicorn. Its coat glimmers with the radiance of dawn, and its eyes shimmer like molten gold. Those who are fortunate enough to witness its arrival are granted a single wish—but not all wishes are as simple as they seem.

Liora had heard the stories since she was a child. She had grown up with tales of the unicorn that appeared once in a lifetime, of the opportunity to wish for anything one's heart desired. Yet as she grew older, her cynicism blossomed. She believed the stories to be just that—stories. Beautiful, whimsical, but not for people like her. People who lived in the real world.

But when the village elders spoke of the unicorn's arrival, when the air seemed to crackle with something unseen, Liora couldn't ignore the pull in her chest. She was standing at the crossroads of her life. She had spent years trapped in a job that drained her, in a relationship that weighed heavy, and in a life that felt stagnant. She knew the signs were there—the celestial alignment, the strange way the wind carried a hint of something golden and ancient. It was real.

And so, Liora found herself standing at the edge of the forest on a night thick with the scent of wildflowers and damp earth, waiting. The full moon hung high above, and the world was still, as if holding its breath. The air shimmered as though the very fabric of reality was stretching, preparing for something extraordinary. Then, through the mist, it emerged.

At first, it was just a silhouette—glowing softly, like a dream coming to life. But as it drew closer, the creature revealed itself in all its glory. The Golden Unicorn stood before her, its golden coat radiant under the moonlight, its mane flowing like liquid sunlight. Its eyes were pools of liquid gold, deep and wise, as if they had seen centuries unfold.

Liora's heart pounded in her chest as she stared at the unicorn, barely able to comprehend what she was witnessing. "You... you are real," she whispered.

The unicorn's voice came not through sound but through the heart, a deep, resonant presence that filled her mind. "Yes, Liora. I am real. And I have come to grant you a wish."

The weight of the moment settled on her shoulders. This was it—the chance to change her life. She had imagined this moment so many times, dreamed of the endless possibilities. Wealth, love, success—what could she ask for? She had spent years caught in the mundane, wondering what it would take to break free.

"I wish for a life of ease," Liora said, her voice trembling with both excitement and fear. "I want to be free from the burdens that have held me back."

The unicorn lowered its head, eyes glowing brighter. "A life of ease," it repeated, as if tasting the words. "A simple wish, yet not without its consequences."

Liora frowned. "What do you mean?"

"Ease, Liora, can be a dangerous thing," the unicorn said, its voice soft but carrying an ancient wisdom. "When life is too easy, we lose the very things that make us human—growth, struggle, the fire that makes us rise from the ashes. What would you sacrifice to live a life without struggle? Would you still know yourself?"

Liora's stomach clenched. She had never thought of it that way. All she had wanted was peace, a way out of the mess she had made of her life. But now, standing in the presence of this creature, she began to understand that her desire for ease had never been the answer. It was the struggle, the effort, the challenge that shaped who she was.

"I... I don't want to lose myself," she whispered, the words hitting her like a wave.

The unicorn nodded gently. "You are wiser than you think. You have come to understand the heart of the matter. The challenge of life is what gives it meaning, not the absence of it. Struggle brings growth, and growth brings wisdom. A wish for ease would rob you of your own power, your own agency."

Liora took a deep breath, her mind swirling with the weight of the unicorn's words. For so long, she had sought the quick fix, the escape from her own unhappiness. She had been afraid to face the difficulties head-on, believing that comfort was the ultimate goal. But now, standing in front of the Golden Unicorn, she saw the truth—ease without growth was an illusion. A life without challenge was a life without depth.

"I wish," Liora began, her voice clearer now, "for the strength to face my challenges. To learn from them, to rise above them, and to become the person I am meant to be."

The unicorn's eyes softened with approval. "A wise wish, Liora. You have chosen not the path of ease, but the path of growth. This is the gift I will give you."

With a single graceful motion, the unicorn lowered its horn toward Liora's chest. The touch was light, but it sent a wave of energy coursing through her body. She felt her heart race, her mind clear, and a new strength fill her being. It was as though a veil had been lifted from her soul, and she saw herself for the first time with true clarity.

"You now have the strength to face your fears," the unicorn said, "and the wisdom to know that the path forward will not always be easy, but it will always be worth it."

As the unicorn began to fade into the mist, Liora stood in awe, feeling a peace she had never known before. She understood now that true freedom came not from avoiding hardship, but from embracing it, learning from it, and becoming stronger with each step. The world would not always be kind, and life would not always be easy, but with the strength she had found, she was ready to face whatever came next.

And as the unicorn disappeared into the night, leaving only the echo of its words behind, Liora realized that the most powerful magic of all was not the granting of wishes, but the ability to shape her own fate.

# The Unicorn's Lullaby

In the valley of Solara, where the rivers gleamed with the colors of the sunset and the hills rose like ancient guardians, lived a unicorn named Lyra. Her coat shimmered like silver under the moonlight, and her horn was a twisted spiral of radiant gold. But what made Lyra unique, even among the many mystical creatures of Solara, was her lullaby.

Lyra had always sung, but it wasn't until she had come of age that she discovered the true power of her voice. Her lullaby was unlike anything the world had ever known. It wasn't just a song—it was a melody woven with the very essence of the earth. When Lyra sang, the flowers bloomed brighter, the rivers ran more smoothly, and the sky seemed to stretch on forever, filled with peace. But most of all, her lullaby soothed restless souls. It calmed the anxious, healed the broken, and restored balance where it had been lost.

Over the years, travelers from distant lands came to hear her sing, seeking comfort, solace, and peace. Lyra never asked for anything in return, her joy came from seeing the world around her calm and content.

But one cold evening, just as the stars began to glitter in the indigo sky, something happened. Lyra was singing her usual lullaby, a soft, ethereal melody that carried across the valley. The winds shifted, the trees swayed gently in time with the music, and for a moment, the world stood still in perfect harmony. But then, as the last note faded into the night, a shadow swept across the land.

Lyra paused, her heart suddenly heavy with an unsettling feeling. From the edge of the forest, a figure appeared—a man cloaked in darkness. His features were obscured, but his presence was undeniable, like the cold breath of winter creeping through the air.

"You sing well, unicorn," the man's voice was smooth, but there was an edge to it, a hint of something sinister. "But it's time for your gift to be of use."

Before Lyra could react, the man raised his hands. A flicker of dark energy surged toward her, and in an instant, her lullaby was silenced. The world around her seemed to freeze, the vibrant colors of the valley drained, leaving only a dull, lifeless gray. She felt a sharp pain in her chest, like something had been torn away from her.

The man laughed as he held up a small crystal, glowing faintly with a dull red light. "Your lullaby," he sneered, "will serve me now. I will take its power and use it to spread chaos, to unravel the peace you so naively hold dear."

With that, he vanished into the night, leaving Lyra alone in the eerie silence. The valley had changed. The peace that had once lived in the air was gone, replaced with an unbearable tension that clung to everything. The trees whispered in fear, and the rivers flowed with a restless current, as if the earth itself was crying out for the lullaby that had been stolen.

Lyra's heart ached as she realized what had happened. The lullaby was not just a song—it was the pulse of the world, a magic that held the balance together. Without it, the chaos would grow. She had to find a way to reclaim her song, to restore the peace that had been so carelessly stolen.

The next days were spent in solitude. Lyra wandered the valley, searching for some trace of the man who had taken her lullaby. She sang softly to herself, but the melodies felt empty, hollow, without the magic that had once filled them. And as the days passed, the world seemed to wither. Flowers no longer bloomed, and the rivers began to dry. The creatures of Solara, once filled with life, wandered aimlessly, lost without the comforting lullaby.

Then, one morning, as Lyra stood at the edge of the river, she felt a presence behind her. She turned to see the man once more, this time standing silently in the distance.

"You've come to take it back, haven't you?" he asked, his voice filled with amusement.

Lyra's heart raced. "Please, give it back. The world cannot function without it. The peace you sought to create through chaos will only destroy everything."

The man smiled darkly. "You misunderstand. I did not steal it for power—I took it because the world needs change. You, and everything you represent, are too pure, too perfect. It's an illusion. I am giving the world something real—freedom from the chains of peace."

Lyra shook her head. "You don't understand. Peace isn't about perfection—it's about balance. Without it, the world falls apart. Chaos is only destruction."

The man's eyes narrowed. "Then let's see if you can prove that."

With a snap of his fingers, he hurled the crystal toward her. Lyra's heart skipped a beat, and before she could react, the crystal shattered, sending a wave of energy through her body. Her vision blurred, and the world around her spun. For a moment, it felt like everything she had ever known was being torn away. She fell to her knees, overwhelmed by the weight of the energy she could no longer control.

But then, something deep inside her shifted. She realized that she had been mistaken. The lullaby, the peace—it was not just a power contained within her. It was a reflection of something much greater, a part of the world itself. And like the river, like the trees, it needed to flow, to change, to evolve. She had been holding on too tightly, trying to preserve something that needed to breathe, to adapt.

Lyra stood, her eyes clearing as she began to sing—not the lullaby as she had known it, but a new song, one that resonated with the very heart of the world. It was a song of transformation, of acceptance. Her voice filled the air, not to calm, but to awaken.

The man stood frozen, his face filled with shock and confusion. The crystal he had stolen began to dissolve, its power unraveling as Lyra's song surged through the air. The earth trembled, and for the first time in days, the sun broke through the clouds, casting light on the valley once more.

"You see?" Lyra said softly, her voice calm now, but filled with understanding. "The lullaby was never meant to be kept locked away. It was meant to grow with the world, to change with it."

The man took a step back, his power waning as Lyra's song enveloped him. With a final look of defeat, he vanished into the wind, his intentions undone by the very peace he had tried to destroy.

As the valley came alive again, Lyra understood the lesson she had learned: peace was not a static state, but a dynamic force, always in motion, always adapting. And in that motion, the world found its true harmony.

# The Unicorn and the Magician

In the heart of a distant land, where the mountains kissed the sky and the forests whispered secrets older than time itself, there lived a powerful magician named Silas. His name was spoken in awe by the common folk and in fear by his rivals, for he had mastered the arts of magic in a way that few could even dream. His powers were vast—he could bend the elements, summon storms, and read the very threads of fate that wove the lives of men. Yet, despite all his skill, there was one thing that eluded him: the magic of the unicorn.

The unicorns, beings of pure light and grace, were creatures of immense power, capable of feats that defied understanding. Their horns, gleaming with ethereal magic, were said to heal wounds, purify poisons, and grant immortality. Many sought them out, but the unicorns were elusive, hiding in the depths of enchanted forests or among the highest peaks, where no mortal could reach them. Silas, however, was determined. He knew that capturing a unicorn's magic would grant him the ability to ascend beyond any other magician, to become more powerful than the gods themselves.

One evening, as the last rays of the sun painted the sky in shades of gold and crimson, Silas ventured deep into the ancient woods that stretched beyond the kingdom. He had studied every spell, every incantation that could lead him to the unicorn. His heart pulsed with anticipation. This was the night he would find what he had sought for so long.

As he trekked deeper into the forest, the air grew thick with the scent of moss and earth, the trees towering above like silent sentinels. In the distance, he saw a glimmering light. It was soft at first, like a star glimpsed through the leaves, but as he approached, the light grew brighter, more defined, until at last, he stood in a clearing bathed in moonlight. And there, standing as if woven from the very light itself, was the unicorn.

The creature was as magnificent as any tale had described. Its coat shimmered like starlight, its eyes glowed with a wisdom that seemed to stretch through the ages, and its horn, long and spiraled, gleamed with an otherworldly radiance. Silas' breath caught in his throat. He had found it—the source of all his desire.

He raised his hands, casting the incantation that would bind the unicorn to his will. His words echoed through the clearing, vibrating with the power of centuries of study. The unicorn did not move, did not flinch, as the magic swirled around it. Silas smiled, believing that he had already won.

But the unicorn's eyes locked onto his, and in that instant, Silas felt the ground beneath his feet tremble. The air grew thick, charged with an energy he had never known, a force that was not his to command. The unicorn lowered its head, its horn glowing brighter, and for a brief moment, Silas felt as if his very soul was being laid bare before it.

"You seek my magic, magician," the unicorn's voice resonated in his mind, calm and clear, as though spoken by the wind itself. "But you cannot possess what is not meant to be owned."

Silas froze, his spell faltering as the unicorn's words washed over him. "You cannot control me," the unicorn continued. "I am not a thing to be captured or bent to your will. My magic is not for greed or for dominance. It is for balance, for harmony."

"But my power—" Silas began, but the unicorn cut him off.

"Your power is a shadow of true strength," the unicorn said. "You seek to conquer, to control, to wield the world like a puppet, but you do not understand what power truly is."

Silas, for the first time, felt doubt. He had spent his life seeking to dominate, to control the forces of nature, to bend them to his whims. He had never considered the consequences of his desires, the imbalance that might come from taking what was never meant to be taken. The unicorn's presence made him feel small, insignificant, and vulnerable in a way he had never known.

The unicorn stepped closer, its eyes never leaving Silas. "Power is not in domination. It is in understanding. In respect. In harmony with the world around you, not against it."

Silas, for all his arrogance, had never truly understood this. He had always viewed the world as something to be controlled, to be shaped by his hands. But now, standing before the unicorn, he saw the world through a different lens, one of unity rather than conquest. The magic he had so desperately sought now seemed like a fleeting illusion, a false promise of satisfaction.

In that moment, the unicorn's magic began to flow—not into Silas, but through him. It filled the air, filling every space between them with an overwhelming sense of peace, of something ancient and eternal. Silas, once so certain of his own power, found himself overwhelmed, humbled by the purity of the magic that surrounded him. It was unlike any force he had ever encountered—a power not to be controlled, but to be felt, experienced, and shared.

The unicorn's gaze softened. "You have sought my magic, but in doing so, you have learned the true lesson. Magic is not something to be owned. It is a force that connects all things. When you learn to respect that connection, you will understand true power."

As the last words faded from his mind, the unicorn turned and walked away, disappearing into the shadows of the forest, leaving Silas standing in the clearing, the magic of the world pulsing softly around him. His heart was heavy, but not with regret—instead, it was filled with an understanding he had never known before. He had sought to take, to control, but in the end, he had been given something far greater: the knowledge of his own limits and the power of respect.

Silas stood in the clearing, the moonlight now bathing the world in a soft glow, and for the first time, he felt at peace. He would no longer seek to dominate or control. He would learn, as the unicorn had taught him, to listen to the world, to the forces that shaped it, and to find strength not in ownership, but in understanding. And as the night wrapped around him, he finally understood what true magic was.

# The Unicorn and the Butterfly

In the heart of the Dreamwood Forest, where the trees whispered age-old secrets and the rivers flowed with laughter, lived a unicorn named Lyra. She was a creature of incredible grace, her coat as white as the moon's reflection in still water, her horn a delicate spiral of iridescent light. Lyra had always seen the world through a lens of grandeur. She reveled in the sweeping vistas, the majesty of the mountains, and the vibrant fields that stretched beneath the endless sky. To her, beauty was something vast and overwhelming—something to be admired from afar, something to be conquered and understood.

One early morning, as Lyra wandered through the dew-kissed meadow, she noticed something unusual—a tiny shimmer in the air. At first, she thought it was a stray beam of sunlight filtering through the trees. But as she drew closer, she realized it was a butterfly, no larger than a leaf, flitting through the air with wings that glowed like fragments of a rainbow. It danced in and out of the soft petals of the wildflowers, its delicate wings beating a soft rhythm in the morning breeze.

Lyra had never seen anything like it before. She had known many creatures in Dreamwood, but this butterfly felt different—magical, even. Curious, she lowered her head, her silvery mane cascading like a waterfall as she approached the butterfly.

"Hello," Lyra said softly, her voice a gentle melody that carried through the air.

The butterfly paused in mid-flight, its wings fluttering as it tilted its head toward the unicorn. It spoke, though its voice was like a soft whisper, a vibration that seemed to echo in Lyra's mind.

"Hello, Lyra," the butterfly replied. "I am Aeria, the keeper of fleeting moments."

Lyra blinked, surprised to hear the butterfly speak. "The keeper of fleeting moments?" she asked, puzzled.

Aeria's wings fluttered again, casting a soft, colorful glow. "I see the beauty in the smallest things—the things others often overlook. I dance between the petals of a flower, the drops of dew on a leaf, the fleeting moment of a breath taken in the quiet dawn. I remind the world that even the tiniest moments are precious."

Lyra stood still, her hooves barely making a sound on the soft earth beneath her. The unicorn had always been attuned to the grand sights of the world—the sweeping horizons, the towering trees, and the majestic rivers. But the tiny things, the small moments that Aeria spoke of, had always seemed insignificant to her. How could something so small matter when the world was full of such awe-inspiring beauty?

"Why do you spend so much time on such little things?" Lyra asked, her voice soft with curiosity. "The grand beauty of the world seems more... important, doesn't it?"

Aeria fluttered closer to Lyra, its wings glowing brighter in the sunlight. "The grand beauty is magnificent, yes," Aeria said, "but the small moments, the ones you might miss in your haste, are the ones that fill the gaps between all the grandeur. Without them, the world would be empty, like a painting without the fine details. I show people the beauty that is hidden in the smallest of things."

Lyra felt a shift in her heart as she considered the butterfly's words. She had always moved through the world with purpose—her eyes fixed on the horizon, her heart set on the next great thing. But now, she realized that she had been overlooking the tiny wonders around her. The soft rustle of the leaves in the wind, the delicate patterns on a spider's web, the way the light danced on the surface of the stream—these things were as much a part of the world's beauty as the mountains and the skies.

Aeria led Lyra through the meadow, showing her the wonders of the small moments. She watched in awe as Aeria danced on the wings of the wind, fluttering from one wildflower to another. The way the petals curved around the butterfly's wings seemed like a delicate choreography. Lyra marveled at how the sunlight caught each tiny droplet of dew, casting rainbows that sparkled like jewels on the tips of the blades of grass. The world, once so vast and overwhelming, now felt intimate, soft, and alive in ways Lyra had never noticed before.

As the day wore on, Lyra found herself slowing down, breathing in the air with a newfound appreciation. She stopped to watch the ants moving busily along the earth, their tiny bodies carrying morsels of food much larger than themselves. She noticed the way the wind shifted the clouds above, creating new patterns with every passing moment. She marveled at the delicate wings of a dragonfly that zipped past her, and the way the trees seemed to sway in time to the rhythm of the earth's heartbeat.

But as the sun began to set, casting a golden glow over the horizon, Lyra realized something. She turned to Aeria, her heart filled with both joy and sadness. "I see now how precious these moments are," she said softly. "But why is it that you, a butterfly, can see them when I, a unicorn, could not?"

Aeria's wings fluttered gently, her glow dimming as the evening light began to change. "Because, dear Lyra, the more you focus on the big picture, the less you notice the small things that make it whole. You are always chasing the next grand thing, the next horizon. But the beauty of life lies not just in what you seek, but in how you see the world around you. It's in the quiet moments between the noise, the stillness within the chaos. That's where the magic lives."

Lyra's heart fluttered with a new understanding. She had always thought of herself as a creature of great purpose, but she realized now that purpose wasn't always found in the grandest of actions. It was found in the quiet, in the space between the grand events, in the fleeting moments that filled the spaces in between.

As the last light of the day faded and the stars began to twinkle above, Lyra looked at Aeria with deep gratitude. "Thank you for showing me this," she said, her voice filled with warmth. "I will never again overlook the small moments. They are as much a part of the world's beauty as anything else."

Aeria smiled, her wings glowing softly in the twilight. "Remember, Lyra, the world is full of magic—not just in the grand gestures, but in the tiniest of things. It is the little moments that make the world whole."

With that, Aeria fluttered into the night, leaving Lyra standing in the meadow, her heart full of new wonder. The magic of the world had always been right in front of her, waiting to be seen, waiting to be felt. She had learned to stop and truly look, and in doing so, she found a beauty far deeper than she had ever imagined.

From that day on, Lyra's heart was open to the small moments of life. She moved through the world with a quiet awareness, seeing the magic in the everyday—a dewdrop on a leaf, the hum of the wind, the gentle rustle of the trees. And in these tiny moments, she discovered the fullness of life.

# The Unicorn's Lost World

Elara had always felt a strange emptiness in her heart, as though there was something she had forgotten, something she had lost long ago. She had lived for centuries, wandering the forests and hills, a creature of beauty and magic, but with each passing year, the weight of her solitude seemed to grow heavier. Her horn shimmered like the light of the stars, her coat gleamed like freshly fallen snow, and yet, in the quiet of the night, Elara would often wonder if she was the last of her kind.

The other unicorns had vanished centuries ago, their existence fading into myth and legend. The stories spoke of an ancient kingdom, a paradise where unicorns had lived in harmony with nature, their magic a force that flowed through the land like a gentle river. But that kingdom was no more, its magic lost to time, and Elara, the last unicorn, had no memory of it.

One evening, as Elara wandered the outskirts of a forgotten forest, something strange happened. The air grew thick with magic, the trees seemed to whisper, and a faint light shimmered in the distance. Elara's hooves carried her forward without thought, her heart racing as she followed the mysterious glow. She passed through a dense thicket of trees, and suddenly, before her, lay an ancient ruin—a stone structure half-buried in moss, its towering walls crumbling with age.

The sight filled Elara with a deep sense of recognition, as though she had seen this place in a dream. The air crackled with power, and she felt a pull deep within her chest, a calling she could not ignore. The magic of the place surged in her veins, filling her with a strange energy. She stepped forward, her hooves echoing on the stone, until she stood at the center of the ruins, where a faded inscription was carved into the stone.

Curious, Elara lowered her head to inspect it, her horn glowing softly in the dim light. As she touched the ancient markings with the tip of her horn, the stone seemed to come alive, the carvings shifting and changing. Words she could not understand filled her mind, a language lost to time. And then, like a sudden gust of wind, a vision washed over her.

She saw a kingdom, vast and beautiful, with fields of golden flowers stretching beyond the horizon. She saw unicorns, their horns glowing with magic, running freely through the meadows, their laughter echoing in the air. But then the vision darkened. The skies turned black, the earth trembled, and a shadow fell over the kingdom. The unicorns fought, their magic clashing against an unknown force, but in the end, they were overwhelmed. One by one, the unicorns fell, their magic fading, their kingdom crumbling to dust.

Elara's heart pounded in her chest as the vision faded, leaving her standing alone in the ruins. The weight of the truth settled over her like a heavy cloak. She was not just the last of her kind; she was the last hope of an ancient kingdom. Her magic, the magic of the unicorns, had been locked away, forgotten, waiting for someone to reclaim it. And now, that someone was her.

She didn't know how, or why, but Elara knew that she had been chosen to restore what had been lost. She had to reclaim the kingdom's magic, to awaken the power that had once flowed through the land and give it new life.

But how could she, a solitary unicorn, possibly do such a thing? Her magic had always been her own, a force that healed and protected, but could it restore an entire kingdom? Could she bring back the magic of her people?

With determination rising in her heart, Elara set out on a journey to unlock the secrets of the ancient kingdom. She traveled through forgotten forests and across wide, barren plains. She encountered creatures who had never seen a unicorn, some who were kind and curious, others who feared her magic. Along the way, she learned to trust herself, to believe in the power that surged through her, even when doubts whispered in the back of her mind.

Finally, after what felt like an eternity, Elara came upon the heart of the kingdom—an ancient temple hidden deep within the mountains. The temple was carved into the rock, its walls covered in runes and symbols that glowed faintly with the last remnants of magic. Elara entered the temple, her steps echoing in the vast chamber. At the center, a stone altar stood, and above it, a great crystal hung suspended in midair, glowing with a brilliant light.

As Elara approached the altar, she felt the power of the crystal calling to her, resonating with the magic that flowed through her own veins. She knew, without a doubt, that this was the source of the kingdom's power, the heart of its magic. And yet, it was silent, dormant, waiting for the right moment to awaken.

Elara closed her eyes and let her horn glow brightly. She focused on the vision she had seen, on the beauty of the kingdom and the strength of her people. She thought of the lives that had been lost, the magic that had been stolen, and the world that had been left in darkness. She poured all of her energy, all of her hope, into the crystal.

For a moment, nothing happened. But then, slowly, the crystal began to pulse, its light growing stronger with each beat. The magic surged through Elara, flowing from her into the crystal, and then outward, flooding the land with a brilliance she had never known. The ground trembled, the air shimmered, and Elara felt a warmth fill her heart as the magic of the unicorns returned to the world.

But as the light faded and the crystal settled, Elara opened her eyes and saw something she hadn't expected. The kingdom's magic had not just been restored—it had transformed. The land, once barren and desolate, now bloomed with life. Flowers grew in abundance, rivers flowed freely, and the sky above gleamed with an ethereal light. But there was something else. Elara realized that the magic of the unicorns was not just in the land, it was in her—she was the living embodiment of the kingdom's power, a beacon of hope for the world.

In that moment, Elara understood the lesson she had learned: she had never been alone. The magic of the unicorns, the power of the kingdom, was never truly gone. It had lived on inside her all along. She had simply needed to believe in herself, to trust in her own strength, to restore what had been lost.

As Elara stood in the heart of the revived kingdom, she knew that the future was no longer uncertain. The magic of the unicorns was alive again, not in some distant past, but in the world around her, in the heart of every creature that called the land home. And she, the last of her kind, had become its guardian.

# Unicorns of the Sea

Far beneath the surface of the ocean, where sunlight barely touches and the waters swirl in perpetual mystery, there lived a species of unicorns unlike any other. These sea unicorns, known as the Aqualis, were creatures of ethereal beauty, their bodies shimmering with the colors of the deep sea—pale blues and greens, iridescent silvers, and flashes of gold. Their horns, long and spiral, were made of living coral, a vibrant fusion of sea life and magic. They were not the graceful, land-dwelling unicorns of myth but beings born of water, entrusted with a duty older than the oceans themselves.

The Aqualis lived in the depths, guarding the ancient treasures hidden beneath the sea: forgotten kingdoms of coral and stone, shipwrecks filled with relics from distant lands, and secrets lost to time. These treasures, however, were not gold or jewels. They were the knowledge of the world, the wisdom of the earth's first civilizations, and the magic that kept the oceans balanced and alive. The Aqualis were the keepers of these wonders, protectors of the deep's most sacred secrets.

For centuries, they had carried out this task without interruption, hidden from the eyes of humankind. The legends of the sea unicorns were nothing more than myths, stories passed down through sailors and fishermen who spoke in whispers of the creatures they swore to have seen, dancing in the moonlight, just beyond the reach of their boats. But to the Aqualis, this was their life—one of quiet vigilance, of solitude and peace beneath the waves.

One such unicorn, a young mare named Ondine, had lived all her life within the coral reefs that surrounded the kingdom's secret gates. The treasure she guarded was a well of ancient magic, a source of power that had once been used to heal the world itself. But now, the magic lay dormant, lost to the ages, and Ondine's only task was to keep the knowledge safe.

Ondine was content. She had no desire to venture beyond the deep, no curiosity for the world above. She had seen it all through the fragments of dreams that reached her as she slept in the quiet of the sea—flashes of ships, of far-off lands, of strange beings walking upon the land. But Ondine was always drawn back to the cool embrace of the ocean, to the soft music of the currents and the shimmering dance of bioluminescent fish.

One day, however, her peace was shattered. She was swimming through the kelp forests, her long mane trailing behind her like a ribbon of silver, when she felt it—a disturbance in the water. It was subtle at first, like the faintest ripple running through the vast ocean. But Ondine's instincts, honed through centuries of guarding the sacred treasure, told her that something was wrong.

As she swam deeper, her heart began to race. The disturbance grew stronger, and soon, she could feel the weight of it pressing down on her. She reached the gate to the ancient treasure—a stone door etched with symbols that no human had ever seen, sealed with the magic of the sea. It was meant to be impenetrable, a barrier that only the Aqualis could approach. But now, there was something pulling at the gate, something unseen, but undeniable.

With a flick of her horn, Ondine channeled the ancient magic of the sea, sending a pulse of energy through the water to reinforce the seal. But it was not enough. The gate shuddered and groaned, and for the first time in centuries, the barrier began to weaken. The sea itself seemed to react, the currents growing fierce, the water swirling in agitation. Ondine's heart thudded in her chest.

From the murky depths, a figure appeared—human, no less. A diver, clad in dark, intricate armor, his eyes wide with a mix of fear and awe as he descended toward the gate. He was not like the sailors she had heard of in her dreams. His presence was not a mere curiosity—it was a disturbance, a force of intent. He was after something, and Ondine could feel the desperation in his every movement.

Before Ondine could act, the diver touched the stone gate. A pulse of energy flared from the point of contact, sending a shockwave through the water. The gate trembled violently, and then, with a sound that echoed like a death knell, the barrier shattered. The treasure—the magic—was now exposed to the world.

Ondine's heart sank. She had failed. The knowledge, the power that had been hidden for eons, was now vulnerable. The diver had unlocked something that was never meant to be touched, never meant to be taken.

She charged toward him, her horn glowing with pure intent. But before she could reach him, the diver turned. His face, hidden behind a mask, betrayed no fear. Instead, his eyes gleamed with triumph. And in his hand, he held a small object—a key, made of coral and sea glass, identical to the one she had been entrusted to protect.

"You've failed," Ondine said, her voice low but resolute. "You don't understand the consequences of what you've done."

The diver's lips curved upward in a smile, but his eyes remained cold. "I understand more than you think. I've been searching for this key my entire life. You think you can keep magic hidden from the world? I will take it, and I will use it to bring power to those who are willing to use it."

Ondine's heart twisted with sorrow. The diver's intentions were clear now. He was not here for peace. He was here for dominance, for control. He sought to harness the magic of the ocean, not to restore it, but to twist it to his own ends. He did not understand the delicate balance of the seas, the sacred duty that the Aqualis had protected for so long.

But Ondine realized something in that moment. The magic of the sea was not meant to be hidden away, hoarded by the Aqualis alone. It was a part of the world, a force that connected all living things.

Perhaps it was time for the world to learn what lay beneath the surface. Perhaps it was time for humanity to understand the power that the ocean held—not to control it, but to protect it.

With a deep breath, Ondine lowered her horn and released a burst of energy—one that wasn't meant to stop the diver, but to show him. The magic of the ocean flowed through her, its vastness and depth seeping into the diver's very soul. She let him feel the weight of the sea, the ancient power that flowed in harmony with the world. And in that moment, something shifted in him. The hunger in his eyes softened, replaced by something more fragile—regret.

The diver slowly released the key, watching as it fell to the depths of the ocean, returning to where it belonged. Ondine turned to the shattered gate, and as she swam toward it, she felt the magic of the sea begin to settle, once again in balance.

The diver remained, his eyes no longer filled with conquest but with something deeper, something quieter. He had learned, as many do, that some treasures are not meant to be claimed, and some magic is too vast to control.

As Ondine returned to the depths, she realized that her task was not to guard the treasure, but to ensure that it was understood—that the magic of the ocean belonged to all who respected it, and that its power was never truly lost, but only waiting to be shared.

# The Unicorn's Footprints

The ancient forest stretched before them, dense and tangled, a labyrinth of towering trees and thick underbrush. A group of explorers—five in total—stood at the forest's edge, their eyes scanning the darkening woods. The last light of the day filtered through the canopy above, casting shadows that seemed to dance with the promise of something hidden, something magical.

At the head of the group was Aidan, an experienced adventurer with a reputation for solving mysteries that others would shy away from. He had spent his career hunting down forgotten treasures, ancient secrets, and hidden worlds, but this was different. The map they had discovered, crumpled and torn, pointed to something far more elusive than gold or relics: the tracks of a unicorn.

"Are we sure this is the right place?" asked Eliza, a young historian with an insatiable curiosity and a skeptical eye. Her fingers tightened around the map, her eyes fixed on the path ahead. "Unicorns? Really? I mean, I know we've all heard the stories, but—"

"A few hundred years ago, this forest was rumored to be the last place where unicorns were seen," Aidan interrupted, his voice steady but tinged with excitement. "And the map we found leads us here, to these exact woods. We follow the trail, and it'll lead us to something incredible."

"I hope you're right," muttered Greg, an engineer who was more accustomed to working with machines than myths. "Because I've got a bad feeling about this."

The group, undeterred by their doubts, pressed on. As they ventured deeper into the forest, the trees grew older, their bark gnarled and twisted, the air thick with the scent of moss and earth. The path was narrow, the ground uneven, but it was the footprints that caught their attention. At first, they thought they had imagined it. But then, the prints appeared again—a series of glowing hoofprints in the dirt, soft yet unmistakable.

"Look!" whispered Eliza, her voice trembling with disbelief. "There, right in front of us."

The prints glowed faintly in the moonlight, their edges shimmering with a light that seemed to pulse with a life of its own. Each step left an imprint that burned bright before fading, leaving only a whisper of light in the air.

"I've never seen anything like this before," Aidan said, his voice low in awe. "It's real. It's happening."

They followed the trail, each print leading them deeper into the heart of the forest, until the trees parted to reveal a hidden valley. The land before them was unlike anything they had ever seen—a lush, verdant meadow filled with glowing flowers and towering mushrooms. The air was warm, thick with the scent of wild jasmine and the hum of a distant stream. And at the center of it all, standing atop a hill, was the creature they had been searching for.

A unicorn. Its coat was as white as freshly fallen snow, its mane cascading in waves of silver and gold. Its horn, long and spiraled, shimmered like a beam of light piercing the darkness. The creature's eyes, pools of liquid amber, locked onto the explorers as they approached, as though it had been waiting for them all along.

For a moment, none of them spoke. They stood frozen, their breath catching in their throats. The unicorn, regal and untamed, stared at them, its presence overwhelming. It was as if the entire world had stopped moving, holding its breath, waiting for something to unfold.

Aidan, always the first to act, took a cautious step forward. "We've followed the trail," he said quietly, his voice barely above a whisper. "We've come for the secrets of this world, for the answers that have been lost."

The unicorn tilted its head, its eyes studying him. Then, without a word, it began to move. Slowly at first, it walked toward the group, its hooves making no sound against the earth. As it passed, a shimmering light enveloped the explorers, and they felt a sudden, inexplicable sense of peace wash over them.

The unicorn stopped just before them, its gaze still fixed on Aidan. With a sudden movement, it lowered its head, and a soft, melodic sound filled the air—a song, like a lullaby, that resonated deep in their hearts. The air shimmered as the light from the unicorn's horn intensified, and a flood of memories, images, and emotions rushed into their minds.

Visions of a world long forgotten played before their eyes: an ancient kingdom of magic, its people living in harmony with the land, protected by the unicorns. The unicorns were the guardians, their magic the very heart of the world. But one day, the kingdom fell—betrayed by those who sought to control the power of the unicorns. The creatures vanished, leaving only the traces of their magic behind.

The vision faded as quickly as it had come, and the group stood in silence. Aidan's mind was reeling, his heart heavy with the weight of what he had seen. The unicorn's song had shown them the truth: the unicorns were not merely mythical creatures—they were the last remnants of an ancient, forgotten kingdom. Their magic had been hidden away, waiting for the right moment to be rediscovered.

"The kingdom," Eliza whispered, "it's gone. All of it."

The unicorn nodded, its expression unreadable. Then, it turned and walked toward a large, smooth stone at the center of the meadow. With a graceful movement of its horn, the stone shifted, revealing a hidden chamber beneath it. A warm light emanated from within, and Aidan's heart skipped a beat as he saw what lay inside.

It was a chest, covered in ancient runes, its surface etched with symbols that seemed to glow with the same magic that surrounded them. The chest was the source of the unicorn's power, the last key to restoring the lost kingdom.

Aidan moved to open the chest, but before he could touch it, the unicorn's voice echoed in his mind, firm and clear. "The magic of the kingdom is not for possession," it said. "It is meant to be shared, to restore the balance of the world. Do you understand this?"

Aidan hesitated, a flash of doubt crossing his mind. He had come for the treasure, for the magic that could change everything, but now he understood. The magic of the unicorns was not to be used for personal gain, nor could it be locked away again. It was a force meant to heal, to restore, to balance the world.

With a deep breath, Aidan stepped back, allowing the unicorn to open the chest itself. Inside was not gold or jewels, but a single glowing crystal, its light pulsing with the same rhythm as the world itself. The unicorn touched the crystal with its horn, and a surge of energy flooded the meadow. The air hummed with the power of the ancient magic, and the explorers felt their hearts swell with a sense of purpose.

As the unicorn turned to leave, its voice filled their minds once more. "The world will heal, but it must be done together. The magic will return, but only if you are willing to share it with the world, not keep it for yourselves."

With that, the unicorn vanished into the night, leaving behind only the shimmering footprints that had led them there. The explorers stood in silence, their hearts full, their mission now clear. The world they had discovered was not one to conquer—it was one to protect, to honor, and to share.

# The Unicorn's Chosen One

The world was on the cusp of change, though no one knew it yet. In the quiet town of Ironswood, nestled between rolling hills and dense forests, lived a young man named Ethan. He was a man of practicality, having inherited a small farm from his father, where he worked tirelessly every day. The village was small, the kind where everyone knew everyone else, and yet, Ethan often felt out of place, as though something more awaited him, though he could not say exactly what that something was. Life was simple, but simple life often leaves a hunger for something undefined.

One evening, as he returned from his usual rounds in the fields, the sun setting low behind the hills, Ethan saw something that stopped him in his tracks. At the edge of the woods, where the trees met the wildflowers, a figure stood watching him. It was a unicorn. Its coat was as white as the moon, gleaming with a strange, ethereal glow. Its long, spiral horn caught the fading light of the sun, casting prismatic colors into the air. For a moment, Ethan thought he had imagined it. Such things were legends, stories for children, nothing more. But as the unicorn stepped closer, its presence undeniable, Ethan knew this was real.

The unicorn moved toward him with grace, and despite the clear divide between their worlds—man and myth—Ethan felt no fear. Instead, a strange peace settled in his chest, as though he had found something he had been searching for, though he didn't know what that was until now.

"You," the unicorn spoke, its voice not with sound, but directly into his mind. It was a deep, resonating presence, filled with an ancient wisdom that made Ethan's breath catch in his throat. "You are the one I have chosen."

Ethan blinked, unsure of what he had heard. "Chosen?" he asked, his voice hoarse, as though the very word carried weight beyond his comprehension.

The unicorn nodded, its gaze unwavering. "Yes. You are the one who will accompany me on a journey, one that will change both our worlds. The balance of magic and man is faltering. Only together can we restore it."

Ethan took a step back. "I don't understand," he said, though he knew, deep within him, that this was no dream. "I'm no hero. I'm just a farmer."

"The world is full of stories about heroes who are called to greatness," the unicorn replied, its voice calm and steady. "But greatness lies not in titles, but in the choices one makes. The world is at a crossroads, Ethan. Magic is fading from the land, and the veil between our world and the otherworld grows thinner by the day. The fates of both are bound together, and you have been chosen because you are not just a man of this world—you are one of both."

Ethan's mind swirled. He had lived his life by the earth, by the seasons and the simple, steady work of tending to crops and animals. He had never thought of himself as anything more. Yet, standing here in the presence of this magical creature, he felt a deep stirring within him—a pull toward something greater, something more than what he had ever known.

The unicorn stepped closer, its horn glowing with a soft light. "Will you come with me, Ethan? Will you embrace your purpose?"

There was no hesitation in his answer. "Yes." It was not something he chose in the moment; it was something he had known deep within him for years. He was tired of the mundanity of life, of feeling as though he had been waiting for something he couldn't name. And now, standing before this creature, he realized that what he had been waiting for was to become something more.

Without another word, the unicorn turned and began walking into the forest. Ethan followed without thinking, stepping off the path and into the unknown.

The journey that lay ahead was not what Ethan expected. The further they traveled, the more the world around them seemed to change. The trees grew taller, their leaves shimmering with colors that didn't exist in nature, and the air grew thick with a magic that pulsed like a heartbeat. They passed through ancient ruins that hummed with forgotten power, crossed rivers that whispered secrets of distant lands, and navigated dark caves where shadows seemed to have a life of their own.

As they journeyed, the unicorn shared stories with Ethan—stories of a time long past when magic and mankind lived in harmony. The unicorn's people had once walked freely among humans, their magic enhancing the world, their presence a force of healing. But something had changed. The balance had tipped, and now, magic was a dwindling force, its power slipping through the cracks of time.

"We were once one," the unicorn said one evening, as they watched the stars above. "The humans who walked beside us were as magical as the land we inhabited. But greed, fear, and ambition corrupted that bond. Now, the magic of our world is fading, and without it, the world will crumble."

Ethan listened intently, his mind racing. He had thought magic was just something from stories. Yet here he was, walking through a world where magic was alive, where it flowed through the very air. The more he learned, the more he understood how fragile this balance was—and how deeply he was now a part of it.

One day, after weeks of traveling, they arrived at a place unlike any other. At the center of a vast, desolate plain, a great tree stood alone. Its bark was blackened, its branches twisted and barren. The air around it was still, and a sense of deep sorrow clung to the very ground beneath their feet.

"This is the heart of the fading magic," the unicorn said, its voice heavy with grief. "The tree once held the essence of our world, but it is dying. And with it, so too is the connection between magic and man."

Ethan stepped forward, drawn by the strange pull of the place. As he approached the tree, something inside him stirred—something deep, ancient, and powerful. He reached out and touched the bark, and in that moment, the ground beneath him trembled. The tree's branches began to move, shifting and groaning as though waking from a long slumber. A flash of light erupted from within the tree, and suddenly, Ethan was no longer standing alone. The air shimmered with the energy of the unicorn's magic, and Ethan felt his own power surge.

The unicorn stood beside him, its eyes filled with both awe and sadness. "You were always part of this world, Ethan," it said, its voice soft. "You are not just a man of this earth. You are the bridge between two worlds, the one who will restore the balance."

Ethan's heart pounded as he realized the truth. He was not merely following a path of adventure. He was the key to restoring what had been lost, the link between mankind and the magic of the world. The world's fate rested on his understanding that both worlds—magic and man—needed each other to survive.

As the light from the tree enveloped them, the unicorn turned to him and said, "The choice is yours, Ethan. You are the chosen one—not because of your strength, but because you understand that it is in the joining, not the separation, that the world will heal."

In that moment, Ethan understood. He was not the hero of the story; he was the one who would heal the rift, not by choosing one side or the other, but by accepting that both magic and man were necessary for the survival of the world. The magic would not return by force, but by understanding, by connection.

And as the first light of dawn broke across the horizon, Ethan made his choice. He stepped forward, into the embrace of both worlds, knowing that his journey was only just beginning.

# The Unicorn's Cave

In the quiet, mist-clad hills of Windserene, a unicorn named Arwen roamed alone. Her coat was the color of moonlight, shimmering faintly in the soft glow of the evening. She had lived a long life, her days filled with a sense of peaceful solitude. Yet, despite the beauty of the land, a constant restlessness gnawed at her heart. She had always known that she was different from the others of her kind, that there was something about her past she couldn't remember, something important, perhaps, lost to time.

Arwen had grown up hearing tales of the ancients, of unicorns who had been the keepers of forgotten knowledge, protectors of an ancient magic that no longer seemed to exist. There was a time, or so the stories said, when unicorns were revered as beings of power, their magic sought after by kings and queens. But that time had passed, and now Arwen wandered, without purpose, lost between what was and what could be.

One crisp morning, as the sun rose in a delicate dance with the clouds, Arwen wandered farther than usual. The dense forest gave way to a cliffside, where the sea roared beneath in rhythmic waves. As she stood on the edge, feeling the wind whip through her mane, something caught her eye. A cave, hidden in the rocks. It was small, almost imperceptible, but there was something about it that drew her in, something that felt... familiar.

Curiosity stirred in Arwen's heart. She stepped closer, her hooves clicking softly against the stone. As she entered the dark mouth of the cave, the air grew cooler, tinged with the scent of salt and ancient earth. Her eyes adjusted to the dim light, and she saw strange symbols etched on the walls, symbols she recognized from the old legends. They spoke of a unicorn who would one day awaken the magic of the ancients, a chosen one who would bridge the gap between the lost past and the uncertain future.

With each step, Arwen felt an increasing sense of urgency, as though she were being guided toward something. The path inside the cave twisted and turned, winding deeper into the mountain. The walls closed in around her, but she felt no fear—only a strange pull that seemed to guide her every movement.

Then, in the heart of the cave, she found it. A large chamber, glowing softly from within, its walls lined with crystals that pulsed with a gentle light. In the center stood a stone pedestal, and upon it lay an ancient scroll, its edges frayed with age. Arwen stepped forward, her breath catching in her chest. She felt as though the very air around her held its breath, waiting for her to reach out and claim what was hers.

Her hooves trembled as she touched the scroll with her horn. The moment she made contact, the chamber seemed to come alive. The crystals flickered brighter, and the symbols on the walls began to glow with an intense light. The voice of the ancients filled her mind—not with words, but with a deep understanding.

The scroll unfurled before her, revealing a prophecy—her prophecy.

"The one who wanders without a name shall find the truth hidden in the earth, and from that truth, the magic of the ancients shall awaken. The chosen one shall rise, but to do so, she must first fall."

Arwen's heart raced. "I am the chosen one?" she whispered to herself. The words, though familiar, felt heavy, as though they were more than just a simple prediction. She felt the weight of destiny settling on her shoulders, as if her entire life had been leading up to this moment.

But there was more.

"To awaken the magic," the voice continued in her mind, "the chosen one must face the truth of her past. She must reconcile the parts of herself that have been lost, and only then will the power of the ancients be hers."

The words echoed through her, stirring something deep within her. A memory, long buried, surfaced—of a time before the world she knew. She saw images of a great battle, of unicorns standing alongside humans, of a betrayal that had shattered everything. And she saw herself, standing amidst it all, a young unicorn full of hope and promise. But then, the vision shifted, and she saw her future, fractured and uncertain. A future where the world was slipping away from the very magic that had once sustained it.

Arwen stepped back from the pedestal, her mind a swirl of confusion. The prophecy had named her the chosen one, but what did it mean? What was the truth of her past that she had to face? The magic of the ancients had always been something to be revered, but now it felt like a burden, a responsibility that might destroy her if she wasn't careful.

As she stood in the chamber, contemplating the weight of her discovery, the crystals around her began to pulse with a stronger rhythm, as though they were reacting to her thoughts. And then, from the darkness of the cave, another presence emerged.

A figure cloaked in shadow, its features obscured by the darkness, stepped toward her. The figure's voice, familiar and haunting, broke the silence.

"You've found it, haven't you?" The voice was calm, yet filled with a strange sense of sorrow. "The truth of your past, and the prophecy of your future."

Arwen's breath caught in her throat. "Who are you?" she demanded, stepping forward.

The figure slowly pulled back the hood of its cloak, revealing a face she never expected to see—hers. It was her own reflection, but twisted, darker, filled with a shadow of sorrow and regret. The other Arwen stepped forward, its eyes filled with an ancient wisdom.

"I am you," the figure said softly. "The part of you that you have forgotten, the part that you buried in order to protect yourself from the truth. You are not just the chosen one. You are the one who betrayed your kind, the one who broke the balance and caused the fall of the unicorns."

Arwen staggered backward, the weight of the revelation crushing her chest. "No," she gasped, shaking her head. "That can't be true. I would never—"

The figure nodded solemnly. "You did. The world fell because you chose power over peace, magic over unity. And now, you must face the truth of what you did. Only then can the magic of the ancients be restored."

The chamber fell silent. Arwen stood frozen, her mind racing. The truth, the real truth, was not just about the magic she could awaken. It was about understanding herself—the parts of her that she had hidden away, the mistakes she had made, and the forgiveness she needed to find. Only through this reckoning would she be able to truly fulfill the prophecy.

As the light of the crystals dimmed and the cave grew quiet once more, Arwen made her choice. She would face her past. She would reconcile the two sides of herself, no matter the cost. Only then would the power of the ancients be hers, and only then would she be able to restore the balance that had been lost.

The unicorn's journey had only just begun.

# Unicorn in the Mirror

Mila had always been drawn to the old, forgotten things. Her home was filled with relics—dusty books, tarnished trinkets, and ancient furniture that smelled of time itself. Her grandmother, a woman of countless stories and secret smiles, had passed down the house to her after she had gone. It was an inheritance wrapped in nostalgia, yet Mila often felt more like a visitor in the rooms, as though the house belonged to a world she could never truly touch.

It was one lazy afternoon when Mila stumbled upon the mirror. It was tucked away in a corner of the attic, behind a pile of boxes stacked with things her grandmother had kept but never spoken about. The mirror was large, framed in dark mahogany, intricately carved with symbols that neither Mila nor her grandmother could ever explain. The glass, though old and clouded with age, still caught the light in an uncanny way, casting strange reflections that made the attic seem colder and more distant than it already was.

Curious, Mila approached the mirror and wiped away the dust from its surface. Her reflection blinked back at her, but there was something different. The room behind her was dim, its usual clutter no longer visible. Instead, she saw an expanse of bright, rolling meadows and forests, stretching out far beyond the glass. The sky was an impossibly bright blue, and a radiant golden light shimmered over everything. And then, there were the unicorns—dozens of them, their coats gleaming with iridescent colors, their spiraled horns catching the light as they grazed peacefully on the land.

Mila gasped, her hand still resting against the frame. She had never seen anything so beautiful. The unicorns moved with grace, their every step like a dance of harmony with the world around them. The air itself seemed filled with a sense of magic, a quiet hum that resonated deep within her chest. The scene felt more real than anything she had ever seen, as though it were unfolding right before her eyes, beyond the boundaries of her own world.

It didn't take long for her to realize—this wasn't just a reflection. The world in the mirror was alive, and it was waiting for her.

Mila stood frozen, staring at the unicorns, her mind racing with questions. How was this possible? Was it some kind of illusion? Or, was the mirror some sort of portal to another world? She had heard tales of mirrors that could show glimpses of other realms, of windows into places where magic still existed, but she had never thought them to be more than stories.

She took a cautious step closer, her breath catching as the unicorns lifted their heads, their eyes meeting hers through the glass. One of them, the largest of the herd, took a slow, deliberate step forward. Its deep, sapphire eyes glistened with intelligence, and its expression seemed almost... inviting.

Without thinking, Mila reached her hand toward the mirror, her fingers grazing the surface of the glass. A soft pulse of energy tingled at her fingertips, and suddenly, she felt the world around her shift. The air grew thicker, warmer. The edges of her vision blurred, and before she could pull away, her hand slipped through the glass, and with it, part of her arm.

Mila gasped, but the moment she tried to pull back, the world inside the mirror seemed to pull her in. Her feet lost contact with the attic floor, and with a sudden rush of air, she was pulled through the glass, tumbling headlong into the world beyond.

The ground beneath her feet was soft, covered in cool grass that seemed to sparkle as if dusted with stardust. The air was crisp and sweet, filled with the scent of wildflowers she had never smelled before. The sky above was vast, stretching endlessly in shades of blue and lavender, with no hint of the mundane world she had known. And before her stood the unicorns, all watching her with that same gentle, knowing gaze.

Mila stood there, her heart racing, taking in the surreal beauty of the scene. The unicorns circled around her, their presence gentle and calming, yet full of an ancient power that pulsed through the very earth beneath her feet. The largest unicorn, the one she had seen before in the mirror, stepped forward, lowering its head in a quiet, respectful bow.

"You have crossed over," the unicorn spoke, its voice like music—soft, melodic, and warm, filling the space around them. "You are the chosen one, the one who can see beyond the veil. But now, you must decide."

Mila stared in disbelief, trying to find her voice. "I don't understand," she whispered. "Chosen? For what? I just—"

The unicorn raised its head, its gaze steady. "The realms are intertwined. Our world and yours are linked by an ancient thread of magic. For eons, our kind has protected the balance, guarding the beauty and purity of life. But now, the balance is slipping. Darkness is creeping into the edges of both worlds, and only one with a pure heart, someone who can see beyond what is, can restore it."

Mila's mind whirled. She had never asked for this. She had never wanted to be the one to save anything, let alone two worlds she didn't fully understand. But the unicorn's words felt undeniable, and for reasons she couldn't explain, Mila knew that this was real. This was hers to face.

The unicorn stepped back, and the herd behind it moved aside, revealing a shimmering path that led up to a glowing pool at the center of a grove. "The path ahead will not be easy," the unicorn continued. "You must decide if you are willing to step fully into this world. If you are, the magic will fill you, and you will be bound to us, to this realm. But remember, once you cross, there will be no turning back."

Mila looked at the unicorn, her chest tight with uncertainty. She glanced back at the mirror, now a distant shimmer behind her. She could almost hear the familiar hum of her own world, the pull of home, but it was faint. There was something here—something extraordinary—that called to her deeper than any familiar place ever could. Yet, the gravity of the decision weighed heavily on her heart. The future she might embrace was unknown, full of both power and responsibility.

"I don't know if I can," she said quietly. "What if I fail? What if the darkness is too strong?"

The unicorn lowered its head, as if understanding her fear. "We all have doubts, young one. But courage is not the absence of fear. It is the willingness to face it and move forward, knowing that even in our smallest actions, we hold the power to shift the balance."

Mila stood still, her mind racing. She felt the power of the unicorns, the weight of their trust. She realized then that her choice wasn't just about saving worlds or facing some grand destiny. It was about becoming who she was truly meant to be. To take that step was to embrace the unknown and accept that, sometimes, the greatest magic lies in the journey itself.

With a final, deep breath, Mila stepped forward, crossing the threshold. The path before her glowed brighter, the world alive with the promise of new beginnings. And as the unicorns surrounded her, their light shining brighter than ever, Mila knew that this world—this new, magical realm—would become her home, where she would face both the greatest challenges and the greatest beauty life could offer.

# The Unicorn's Heart

In the heart of the misty mountains, where the sun barely touched the land and the wind whispered ancient secrets, there lived a unicorn named Solara. Her coat was as white as snow, and her horn gleamed like polished silver. She was unlike any other creature in the realm, for within her chest, beneath her ribcage, lay a heart not of flesh, but of magic—a heart that pulsed with the power of the universe, a rare and ancient magic that had been passed down through generations of unicorns. It was said that whoever possessed the unicorn's heart would wield the power to shape the very fabric of reality.

For centuries, the unicorns had kept their hearts hidden, guarding them fiercely against those who would seek to exploit their power. Solara, however, had lived peacefully in her sanctuary, untouched by greed and desire. The magic of her heart flowed through her, calming the land, healing the sick, and fostering harmony among the creatures of the world. She never sought attention, and in her solitude, she believed her heart's power was enough to keep her world safe.

But not all were content to let her be.

Far to the west, in the shadow of a crumbling kingdom, a band of ruthless villains had heard whispers of the unicorn's heart. Led by a cunning sorcerer named Malcor, they were willing to do whatever it took to claim the heart's power for themselves. Malcor's ambition knew no bounds, and with his twisted followers, he had searched the land for centuries, gathering dark artifacts and spells to aid him in his quest. He believed that with the unicorn's heart, he would be able to overthrow kingdoms and bring the world under his control.

One stormy evening, as lightning split the sky and thunder rattled the earth, Malcor and his followers tracked Solara's location to her sanctuary. The wind howled around the mountaintops as they crept closer to the unicorn's resting place, their eyes glowing with greed. The sorcerer had known that the journey would be perilous, but he cared not for the dangers. His thirst for power drowned out all concern.

When they reached the entrance to Solara's sanctuary, a great stone archway, Malcor stepped forward, raising his hand to cast a spell. His voice, sharp and cruel, filled the air as dark energy surged from his fingertips. The ground trembled beneath him, and a black mist spread out, shrouding the entrance in shadow.

Inside, Solara stirred, sensing the intrusion. Her heart pulsed with a soft, rhythmic glow, and she knew that the time had come to defend the magic she had guarded for so long. She had always known that there would be those who would come for her heart, but she had hoped it would never come to this—hope was a fragile thing, and the greed of men was insatiable.

With a graceful movement, Solara rose from her resting place and stepped into the clearing just outside her sanctuary. Her silver horn glowed with the light of the moon, and her eyes, deep pools of wisdom, locked onto the approaching figures.

Malcor, sensing her presence, sneered as he saw her emerge from the mist. "The unicorn herself," he hissed, his voice dripping with malice. "Give me your heart, Solara, and I will spare your life. Fight me, and your death will be slow and painful."

Solara's voice, calm and steady, broke the silence. "You cannot take what does not belong to you, Malcor. My heart is not a prize to be claimed."

"Then you leave me no choice," Malcor spat, and with a gesture, he unleashed a wave of dark magic that shot toward the unicorn. The magic crackled in the air, twisting the landscape, but Solara stood firm. Her horn glowed brighter, and the dark magic shattered like glass against the power of her light. She charged toward Malcor, her hooves striking the ground with the force of a storm, her heart's magic radiating outward in a pulse of radiant energy.

The villains scattered, their faces twisted in fear and anger. But they had underestimated Solara. She was no mere creature of beauty—she was the embodiment of the earth's magic, and her heart was not a source of destruction, but of creation. With each step she took, the ground healed beneath her hooves, and the sky cleared above her.

Malcor, however, was relentless. He raised his hands to summon another wave of magic, more powerful than the last, but just as he was about to strike, something unexpected happened. The magic in the air shifted. The wind began to swirl around Solara, and her heart's glow intensified, but this time, something new emerged—a connection between the unicorn and the sorcerer. Their magic intertwined, not in conflict, but in balance.

Solara's heart pulsed once more, not as a weapon, but as a force of understanding. Her magic began to fill the air, not to fight, but to heal the rift between them. She had spent her life guarding her heart, believing that it was the source of all that made her special, all that made her important. But in that moment, she realized that it was not the heart alone that held the power—it was the connection between all things, the understanding that even the darkest forces could be touched by light if only they allowed it.

As Malcor's dark magic began to wane, his face twisted in confusion. He had not expected this. He had expected to take, to control, to dominate. But the more he fought, the more Solara's light enveloped him, not in aggression, but in acceptance.

"You seek power, but you do not understand it," Solara's voice echoed through his mind. "Power is not in control. It is in understanding. It is in harmony."

With a final surge of energy, Solara's magic engulfed Malcor, but not in a destructive burst. Instead, the energy wrapped around him like a cocoon, a gentle but unyielding force. For a moment, the sorcerer froze, his body still as though suspended in time. When the light faded,

Malcor fell to his knees, his eyes wide in realization. The greed that had consumed him was gone, replaced by an understanding of something greater, something beyond his reach.

As the villains fled in fear, their master broken, Solara stood tall. She had not destroyed, but instead, she had transformed. She had shown them that true power lay not in the taking of what was not theirs, but in the giving of what was freely shared.

As Solara turned to leave, she felt her heart's magic resonate, not just in her chest, but in the world around her. The land had been healed, not through force, but through understanding. She knew now that her heart was not just a source of power—it was a bridge, a light in the darkness, a reminder that true magic was never meant to be hoarded.

And as she disappeared into the mist, the lesson lingered: that the greatest strength lies not in what we possess, but in how we use what we have to bring balance to the world.

# The Magical Unicorn Parade

Every year, the skies above the Vale of Loria lit up with the sparkling lights of the Unicorn Parade, an event so grand that even the stars seemed to dim in its presence. Unicorns from all corners of the world gathered to celebrate the ancient magic that bound them to the earth, to the stars, and to each other. It was a day of revelry, of unity, where they would parade through the skies in a procession that mesmerized all who were lucky enough to witness it.

For decades, the parade had followed the same pattern: the unicorns would gather at the Great Meadow, their bodies aglow with stardust, their horns casting luminous trails of magic through the night sky. The people of the realm would gather below, their hearts filled with awe and wonder as they watched the mythical creatures glide effortlessly through the air. It was a symbol of peace, of strength, of magic preserved through the ages.

But this year, things were different.

In the weeks leading up to the parade, rumors began to spread among the unicorns. Something was stirring in the dark corners of the realm. Whispers of a curse, an ancient grudge, a betrayal long forgotten, reached the ears of the council that oversaw the unicorns' sacred traditions. Elders spoke of a rift, a crack in the magical barrier that kept the balance of the worlds in harmony. Yet, none of them could have predicted what would unfold when the unicorns gathered on that fateful night.

As the moon rose high in the sky, casting a silvery glow over the Vale, the unicorns began to assemble. Their coats shimmered, their eyes filled with excitement, their horns gleaming like the first light of dawn. Among them was Lyra, a young unicorn whose bright spirit and untested courage had earned her a place in the parade. She had always dreamed of this moment—of soaring through the skies, of dancing among the stars, of feeling the collective magic of her kind fill the air. But tonight, her heart was heavy with an unfamiliar sense of unease.

The ground beneath her hooves hummed with an unusual energy, and she could feel it reverberating through her entire body. It was as though the magic that once flowed so freely through the earth was now strained, stretched thin, and she was not the only one who felt it. The other unicorns were uneasy too, exchanging nervous glances as they formed ranks for the procession.

As the parade began, the unicorns lifted off into the sky, their hooves barely touching the ground as they ascended, trailing clouds of sparkling magic in their wake. The air was thick with the sweet scent of flowers and the soft rustling of wings. Lyra felt the familiar rush of joy as the wind swept through her mane, but the deeper sense of dread never left her. The stars, usually so bright, flickered oddly in the distance, like a heartbeat that was weakening.

And then, as the parade reached its peak—when the unicorns were at the height of their flight, spinning and twirling in elegant formation—something snapped.

At first, it was a subtle thing. A faint tremor in the air. Then, the sky darkened. The stars vanished one by one, as though they were being swallowed by the very fabric of the night. The unicorns' magic faltered, their glow flickering in and out. Lyra gasped, looking around in confusion. The magical threads that had always bound the parade together began to unravel, sending shockwaves through the air.

Before she could make sense of what was happening, a roar echoed from below, shaking the earth beneath her hooves. A massive shadow rose from the ground, towering over the unicorns. It was a creature unlike anything she had ever seen—an enormous beast of dark tendrils and cracked stone, its eyes glowing with malicious intent. The creature roared again, and the air seemed to freeze, the very magic of the unicorns suddenly nullified by the beast's presence.

The unicorns scattered in panic, their graceful formations shattered. Lyra's heart raced as she tried to regain control of her flight, but the creature's presence loomed larger, its energy suffocating. The stars above were gone, and the once bright moon was now hidden behind a veil of dark clouds.

"What's happening?" Lyra cried, her voice trembling as she watched the other unicorns struggling to maintain their balance.

"An ancient curse," a voice called out from the shadows. It was Rilan, the eldest and most respected of the unicorn elders. He had been watching the chaos unfold from a distance, his eyes filled with sorrow. "This was foretold. The parade was meant to be a celebration of unity, but something broke, something that should never have been tampered with."

"What do you mean?" Lyra asked, her voice barely audible above the creature's growls.

"It was a betrayal long ago," Rilan explained, his voice carrying the weight of centuries. "The unicorns, in our wisdom, forged a pact with the realms beyond—both magical and mortal. But in our pride, we grew too confident. We broke the pact, broke the balance. The curse was set in motion, and it has finally caught up with us."

Lyra's mind raced as the words sank in. The curse, the imbalance—it was all her fault. She had taken part in the celebration without understanding the weight of what was at stake. She had joined the parade, believing that magic could fix everything, that the world could remain whole if only the unicorns continued to parade in the skies. But the truth was far more complicated. The magic they had once shared with the world was fragile, and now it was unraveling.

She turned to the creature that towered over them, its tendrils of darkness writhing and twisting in the air. It was feeding off the imbalance, growing stronger with every second. Lyra realized then that the only way to restore the balance—to save the parade and the worlds connected to it—was to make a sacrifice. The magic of the unicorns had always been tied to the hearts of their kind. If she could reach the core of the curse, if she could connect her heart to the creature's darkness, perhaps she could mend what had been broken.

With trembling hooves, Lyra dove toward the beast, her heart pounding in her chest. As she neared it, the air grew colder, the darkness more suffocating. But she did not turn back. She pressed forward, her horn glowing with a quiet, steady light.

And in that moment, she understood. The magic was not in the parade, nor in the rituals they had practiced for so long. It was in the willingness to face what they had broken, to acknowledge their mistakes, and to make them right.

Lyra touched her horn to the creature, and everything went still.

A blinding light exploded outward, sweeping across the sky, pulling the curse back into the depths from which it had come. The darkness vanished, the stars returned, and the moon shone bright again. The parade, broken but not lost, began to reform, the unicorns gathering once more in the sky, their hearts lighter and their magic stronger than before.

The lesson was clear: magic was not something to be celebrated lightly or taken for granted. It was a gift, a responsibility—one that could only thrive in balance. And only through understanding, humility, and sacrifice could that balance be restored.

# The Dreamweaver and the Unicorn

For as long as she could remember, Elara had been a dreamweaver. In the quiet of the night, while the rest of the world slept, she would sit at her window and weave the threads of dreams into intricate patterns that danced in the minds of others. Some dreams were simple—an afternoon picnic, a forgotten conversation. But others were more complex, filled with visions of far-off lands, mythical creatures, and impossible journeys. To her, dreams were not just fleeting images; they were living, breathing entities, waiting to be shaped into something beautiful or dangerous, something magical or mundane.

Her ability had always been a gift. It was a gift she had learned to control, to fine-tune, shaping the dreams of those who sought her out with the precision of an artist working on a canvas. Yet, she had never fully understood the power she wielded. There was one rule she had always followed—never interfere too much, never create something that could disturb the natural course of the dreamer's mind. Her work was delicate, and too much influence could have dire consequences. Still, there was a nagging curiosity in her, a question that she had never dared ask: what if she could shape a dream for herself, a dream that was not bound by the limits of her craft?

One evening, as Elara sat by her window, the world outside cloaked in the velvet blue of twilight, she allowed her mind to wander. She had woven countless dreams for others, but tonight, she wanted to create something for herself. She closed her eyes, reaching into the fabric of her imagination, and began to spin a dream. She wanted something different—something beyond the realms of ordinary dreams. She wanted a creature of beauty, something from the ancient stories that she had always loved. A unicorn, with a silvery mane, a spiraling horn, and eyes that shimmered like the stars. She imagined it as vividly as she could, watching it dance in the fields of her mind.

As she wove the final thread, she felt a strange sensation, as though the dream were alive, pulsing with energy. But when she opened her eyes, nothing had changed. The room was still dark, the only light coming from the faint glow of the moon. Yet, as she glanced back toward the corner of her room, she froze. Standing there, in the middle of her quiet apartment, was the very unicorn she had just imagined.

Elara's heart skipped a beat. She rubbed her eyes, sure that fatigue was playing tricks on her. But the creature remained, its hooves delicately touching the wooden floor, its coat as white as the moonlight streaming through the window. It was real. She could feel its presence, the magic it radiated, filling the space around her. The unicorn's eyes met hers, calm and knowing, as though it had been waiting for her to notice.

"How—how are you here?" Elara whispered, her voice trembling with disbelief.

The unicorn lowered its head, its horn shimmering in the low light. A soft voice echoed in her mind, like a distant song. "You called me," it said. "You wove me from the threads of your dreams, and so I came."

Elara took a hesitant step forward, unsure of what to do. "I didn't mean to— I just wanted to create a dream. I never thought... I never thought you would actually—"

"Dreams are more powerful than you know," the unicorn interrupted, its voice gentle yet firm. "You have the ability to shape worlds, to summon what your heart desires, whether you know it or not. You are a dreamweaver, but now you must learn what it means to weave a reality."

Elara felt a shiver run through her. The weight of the unicorn's words settled in her chest, but she was both terrified and intrigued. She had always kept her dreams carefully contained, never allowing them to spill over into the waking world. But now, she had done exactly that, and the result was standing before her. The unicorn was no longer a figment of her imagination—it was flesh and blood, real and alive.

"Why me?" Elara asked, still struggling to comprehend the situation. "Why now?"

The unicorn's eyes softened. "You have been weaving dreams for others for so long that you've forgotten how to dream for yourself. Your heart is full of untapped power, a potential that has been waiting to be unlocked. I am here to help you understand that power, to show you the consequences of your creations."

Before she could respond, the unicorn turned toward the window and trotted over to it. "Come," it said, its voice echoing in her mind once more. "There is much for you to see."

With a deep breath, Elara followed, her pulse quickening. As she stood beside the unicorn, the room around them seemed to fade away, and the world outside the window shimmered with light. The night sky stretched out before them, and beneath the stars, she saw a landscape unlike anything she had ever seen before. Fields of wildflowers swirled in the wind, mountains rose like giants in the distance, and a river of silver light wound through the land. It was the world she had created in her mind—the world she had woven in her dream—but it was more than just an illusion now. It was alive, breathing, and vast.

"This is what you have called into being," the unicorn said, turning back to her. "This is the reality of your dreams. But remember, all creations have consequences."

Elara looked around in awe, but there was a nagging feeling in her chest. She had created beauty, but was there something more to her dreams that she hadn't yet understood? As the unicorn spoke again, its voice tinged with sadness, she realized that the world she had woven was not without its shadows.

"Every dream holds the potential for both light and dark," the unicorn said. "You have brought me here, but you must now take responsibility for the world you have created. The line between what is real and what is dreamed is thinner than you think."

Elara looked around again, and this time, she noticed the cracks. The flowers withered in places, and the river's shimmering surface darkened. The sky, once full of stars, seemed to flicker, as if it were losing its stability. She had created a world of beauty, but there were flaws, imperfections—things she hadn't intended.

"What have I done?" Elara whispered.

The unicorn lowered its head, its horn glowing with a soft, reassuring light. "What you have done is the beginning. Dreams are not perfect, but they are always evolving. You have the power to reshape them, to heal what has been fractured. But it is up to you to decide what kind of world you want to live in."

With those words, the unicorn stepped back, fading into the mist of the dream world it had come from. The magic around Elara began to shift, and the world around her started to change. She had created the dream, but it was no longer just hers. It was a part of the waking world now, and with that came responsibility.

The next morning, as the first rays of sunlight touched her window, Elara awoke in her bed. The dream was gone, but the lesson lingered. She had called forth the unicorn, and in doing so, had learned that dreams, while beautiful, must be handled with care. They were not just fleeting fantasies; they were a reflection of the power she held within herself, waiting to shape the world around her. And with that power, came the choice to create not just beauty, but balance.

# Unicorn in the Garden

Harlan had always been a man of simple pleasures—freshly tilled soil, the smell of earth after rain, the feel of a rake gliding smoothly through garden beds. He had spent most of his life tending to the modest garden behind his little cottage on the outskirts of town, a haven of vibrant flowers and fragrant herbs. People from the village often marveled at how his flowers bloomed with such brightness and vitality, and Harlan, ever the humble gardener, would smile and shrug, as if the garden took care of itself.

But the truth was, the garden was his sanctuary. It was his escape from the world—a place where he could lose himself in the rhythm of planting, pruning, and harvesting. He had never been married, nor did he have any family left. A few old friends remained in town, but they were busy with their own lives. His interactions with the world outside the garden were brief and often perfunctory.

One morning, while tending to his rose bushes near the far corner of his garden, Harlan noticed something odd. A patch of flowers in a secluded area of the garden, one that had always been calm and still, had begun to shimmer under the sunlight. He leaned in closer, puzzled, and saw what looked like a trail of glistening footprints leading into the thickest part of the flower bed. His heart raced a little as his mind wandered to impossible thoughts—was it some sort of trick of the light? Or something more?

But as he crouched low to inspect the tracks, a sound broke the silence—a soft, melodic whinny, almost like a whisper in the wind. His eyes snapped up, and there, partially hidden beneath a cluster of wild irises, he saw it. A unicorn. Its coat shimmered like silver, its mane glowed with soft hues of violet and blue. The creature stood still, its large, intelligent eyes fixed on him, yet it made no move to flee.

Harlan's breath caught in his throat. He had heard tales of such creatures as a boy—legends spoken in hushed tones by the village elders—but he had never thought to believe in them. And yet, here it was, standing before him, more magnificent than any story could capture.

He reached out a trembling hand, but the unicorn flinched slightly, as if unsure of his intentions. Harlan withdrew his hand slowly, giving the creature the space it seemed to crave. It took a cautious step forward, and with a soft nicker, it nudged the ground beside him, a subtle invitation. He smiled, his heart swelling with a mixture of awe and disbelief.

The unicorn lowered its head, and Harlan marveled at the way the sunlight seemed to dance off its silken coat. He had heard of creatures that could make plants bloom with just their presence, but he had never imagined seeing one for himself. The flowers surrounding them seemed to bloom even more vibrantly in the presence of the creature, as if responding to its magic.

For a long moment, Harlan and the unicorn simply regarded each other in silence. There were no words to be said, no need for them. The garden felt alive with an energy he had never before experienced, as though the land itself was humming in resonance with the creature's presence.

The unicorn took another step closer, and this time, Harlan did not hesitate. He gently reached out, brushing the soft fur along its neck. The unicorn made no protest, only closing its eyes for a brief moment as though savoring the touch. It was then that Harlan realized how truly lonely he had been. The garden had always been his only companion, but this creature—this magical being—was something else entirely. It was a presence that filled the space with a profound sense of peace.

But as the moment stretched on, a sudden chill ran through the air. Harlan pulled back his hand and looked around, uneasy. The sun was beginning to dip lower in the sky, and the peaceful atmosphere had shifted. He sensed something was wrong. The unicorn, too, seemed to sense it, its head lifting as it stepped away from him, its eyes darting nervously to the edges of the garden.

Harlan stood up, his pulse quickening. The sound of footsteps approached—heavy, deliberate. He recognized the distinct tread of people from the village. Panic rose within him. The unicorn's presence was a secret, a fragile thing, and he could not risk the villagers discovering it. They would not understand. The fear, the anger, the need to control—they would want to capture the unicorn, to use it for their own gain. It had happened before, in other places, he knew. People were too curious, too greedy to leave such magic alone.

Without thinking, Harlan stepped forward and placed his hand gently on the unicorn's side. "You have to go," he whispered, his voice tight. The unicorn hesitated, its eyes searching his face. For a brief moment, he thought it might resist, might stay in defiance of the outside world that threatened to disturb its peace. But the unicorn seemed to understand, and with a final glance, it turned, slipping silently into the thickest part of the garden, disappearing into the undergrowth as though it had never been there.

Harlan stood in the quiet, listening to the footsteps grow louder as the villagers approached. He quickly began to tidy up the area, brushing away any evidence of the unicorn's presence, praying they would never find out.

When the villagers arrived, they saw nothing unusual. Only Harlan, standing among his flowers, the serenity of the garden restored. They spoke of the weather, of crops and harvests, and of the mundane matters of daily life. Harlan listened, offering polite responses, all the while his mind racing. His heart longed for the unicorn's return, but he knew he could not allow it. The magic of the garden, of the unicorn, was fragile, and it was his duty to protect it—no matter the cost.

As the sun finally set and the villagers left, Harlan stood alone in the fading light. He walked to the far corner of his garden, where the unicorn had been, and knelt to the ground. There, nestled among the flowers, was a single, delicate silver feather, shining in the moonlight. A token, a reminder that the magic of the unicorn had not truly left, only hidden, waiting to return when the time was right.

The lesson was clear. The unicorn had shown him the beauty of magic, the power of connection, and the depth of his own loneliness. But sometimes, to protect what is most precious, one must let go. The secret of the unicorn, like the garden, would remain hidden for now, preserved in silence and solitude—where it belonged.

# The Return of the Unicorns

For centuries, the unicorns had been hidden, their existence known only in myth and whispered tales. The once-glorious creatures that roamed the earth, their horns sparkling like stars and their coats shining like the moon, had vanished into the shadows of time. The world had forgotten them, or so it seemed. Yet, there were some who still believed in the legends, some who carried the stories of their grace and beauty in their hearts. One such person was Elysia, a historian with a love for ancient lore, who had always suspected that the unicorns weren't just myths. They had once existed, and they would again.

It began on an ordinary morning. Elysia was walking through the forest near her cottage, her mind preoccupied with the texts she had been studying. There were whispers in the ancient books, references to the unicorns and their hidden retreat, but no one had ever truly understood where they had gone or why. She had long thought the unicorns had retreated into some distant, unreachable realm, hidden by magic so powerful it had erased them from human memory.

But that morning, something felt different. As she walked, she noticed the air growing heavier, the silence deeper. The birds seemed to stop singing, the trees standing still as if holding their breath. Elysia paused, her heart racing. Then, she saw it. A flash of light—a glimmer that danced between the trees like a fleeting star. It wasn't just light; it was magic, undeniable and ancient. The hairs on her neck stood on end as she slowly approached the source.

Through the dense foliage, a creature emerged. At first, Elysia thought it was a trick of the light, but as it stepped into the clearing, her eyes widened in disbelief. A unicorn, its body glowing with an ethereal light, its horn like a twisted spiral of silver, stood before her. Its coat shimmered in the sunlight, and its mane seemed to flow like water. For a long moment, neither of them moved. The unicorn, too, seemed to be studying her, its eyes filled with something ancient—wisdom, pain, and perhaps even hope.

"You are real," Elysia whispered, her voice trembling.

The unicorn nodded, its expression calm but resolute. "Yes, we are real. We have always been real, though we have been hidden for far too long."

Elysia's breath caught in her throat. "But why? Why did you disappear?"

The unicorn took a step forward, its hooves making no sound on the soft earth. "The darkness that once sought to destroy us drove us into hiding. The world was not ready for us, and we were not strong enough to face the forces that sought our extinction. For centuries, we have waited, hidden away from the world, growing weaker with each passing generation."

"Darkness?" Elysia repeated, confusion filling her voice. "But what forces? What happened?"

The unicorn's eyes darkened for a brief moment, as if recalling a painful memory. "Once, the unicorns were the protectors of the world's magic, guardians of the balance between light and dark. But greed, fear, and the desire for control spread across the lands. Those who sought power began to fear us, for our magic was pure and untamable. They hunted us, driven by their need to possess what they could never understand. And so, we withdrew, hoping the world would forget us and we could heal in silence."

Elysia felt a pang of sorrow for the unicorn. "That's terrible. But if you've been hiding all this time, why return now? Why come back?"

The unicorn's gaze grew even more intense. "The world has changed. The darkness we once fled from is growing stronger again. It has taken root in places where it was once banished, and now, it threatens to consume the world entirely. We can no longer hide. We must return, confront it, and restore the balance that has been lost."

Elysia's heart pounded. She knew the stories—stories of greed and corruption, of powers seeking to control nature itself. She had heard of the dark forces rising in the east, in the kingdoms where magic was being twisted for power. But she had never imagined the unicorns would return to fight it.

"But you're only one," Elysia said, glancing around. "How can you defeat such a force alone?"

The unicorn smiled faintly, but there was no humor in its eyes. "I am not alone. We are never alone. There are others like me—others who have been hiding, waiting for the right moment to rise. But we cannot do this alone. We need the help of those who still believe, those who have kept the memory of the old magic alive."

Suddenly, the ground beneath them trembled, and the trees groaned in response. A shadow moved across the clearing, growing larger, darker. From the depths of the forest, another figure emerged—another unicorn, larger and darker than the first. Its coat was no longer pure white, but a deep charcoal, its horn crackling with dark energy. It was not evil, but it was corrupted, twisted by the same darkness that had once driven the unicorns into hiding.

The two unicorns locked eyes. The light and the shadow stood facing one another, a silent understanding passing between them. The dark unicorn stepped forward, and the first unicorn, the one Elysia had encountered, bowed its head in respect.

"This is the beginning," the unicorn said softly, turning to Elysia. "The darkness is not merely an external force. It is a part of us, of the choices we have made, of the power we have allowed to grow unchecked. We must confront it, both within ourselves and in the world around us. The return of the unicorns is not just the return of magic—it is the return of balance, and that balance must be fought for, no matter the cost."

Elysia's mind swirled. She had always believed in magic, in the stories her grandmother had told her, but she had never imagined she would be a part of something so vast, so important. She looked at the unicorns, standing side by side, one light, one dark, but both powerful in their own right. They were not just protectors; they were symbols of a balance that had been lost, a reminder of the forces that shaped the world.

"You must choose," the light unicorn said, its voice firm. "Will you stand with us? Will you help restore what has been broken?"

Elysia hesitated, her heart racing. The world outside was changing, the darkness growing stronger, and she knew that standing on the sidelines was no longer an option. She had spent her life learning about the past, but now she had the chance to shape the future. The unicorns had returned, but they needed more than just belief—they needed action.

"I will help," Elysia said, her voice steady despite the fear that gripped her chest. "I'll do whatever it takes."

The unicorns nodded, their eyes filled with quiet gratitude. They knew that the battle ahead would be long, and the stakes higher than ever. But with Elysia's help, they could fight for the balance the world so desperately needed.

As the two unicorns vanished into the mist, Elysia stood alone in the clearing, the weight of her decision settling in her bones. She had taken the first step toward restoring the world, but she also understood that it was only the beginning. To fight the darkness, they would need more than just power—they would need unity, trust, and the strength to confront both the light and the shadow within.

And with that, Elysia knew that the unicorns' return was not just a battle for magic—it was a call for the world to remember its roots, to heal, and to find balance again.

# Get Another Book Free

We love writing and have produced many books.

As a thank you for being one of our amazing readers, we'd like to offer you a free book.

To claim this limited-time offer, visit the site below and enter your name and email address.

You'll receive one of our great books directly to your email, completely free!

**https://free.copypeople.com**

Did you love *Unicorn Magic Discovering the Wonders of a Hidden World*? Then you should read *Realm of Enchantment Tales from the Mystic Lands*[2] by Morgan B. Blake!

[3]

Dive into the enchanting world of *Realm of Enchantment: Tales from the Mystic Lands*, a captivating collection of short stories that whisk you away to realms where magic thrives, mythical creatures roam, and extraordinary adventures await. Each tale unfolds a unique journey through the mystical landscapes of ancient forests, hidden valleys, and fabled cities, where young heroes and seasoned adventurers confront their fears, discover their true selves, and learn the importance of connection and courage.

In this enchanting anthology, you'll encounter:

A spirited young witch mastering her powers to protect her coven. A

---

2. https://books2read.com/u/bPdNYl

3. https://books2read.com/u/bPdNYl

brave explorer navigating treacherous mountains in search of the legendary lost city of gold. An ancient dragon guarding a portal to another realm, testing the mettle of those who seek it. A magical tapestry that reveals glimpses of the future, guiding a young woman on her quest for identity. A hidden valley filled with mythical beings, where the true treasures lie in the bonds of community.

With rich prose and vivid imagery, *Realm of Enchantment* invites readers of all ages to embrace the wonders of imagination and the lessons learned from each journey. Perfect for lovers of fantasy, adventure, and the timeless battle between light and dark, this collection will leave you longing for more.

Embark on an unforgettable adventure where every story teaches us that magic is not just a force to be wielded, but a path to understanding our deepest desires and fears. Join us in the *Realm of Enchantment*, where every turn of the page reveals a new wonder waiting to be discovered.

# Also by Morgan B. Blake

**The Hidden Truth**
Silent Obsession

**Standalone**
Temporal Havoc
The AI Resurrection
99942 Apophis
The Shadows We Keep
Whispers of the Forgotten
Christmas Chronicles: Enchanted Stories for the Holiday Season
Realm of Enchantment Tales from the Mystic Lands
The Taniwha's Secret
Unicorn Magic Discovering the Wonders of a Hidden World

Milton Keynes UK
Ingram Content Group UK Ltd.
UKHW030948261124
451585UK00001B/122